BLUE

B L U E

Joyce Moyer Hostetter

CALKINS CREEK
Honesdale, Pennsylvania

Library of Congress Cataloging-in-Publication Data

Hostetter, Joyce.
Blue / Joyce Moyer Hostetter.—1st ed.
p. cm.
Summary: When teenager Ann Fay takes over as "man of the house" for her
absent soldier father, she struggles to keep the family and herself together in
the face of personal tragedy and the 1940s polio epidemic in North Carolina.
[1. Poliomyelitis—Fiction. 2. Race discrimination—Fiction. 3. Friendship—
Fiction. 4. North Carolina—History—20th century—Fiction] I. Title.
ISBN 978-1-59078-389-4 (alk. paper)
Pz7.H81125 Bl 2006
[Fic]—dc22

2005033570

Quotations have been taken from 1944 and 1945
issues of the *Hickory* [N.C.] *Daily Record.*
Reprinted with permission.

CALKINS CREEK
An Imprint of Boyds Mills Press, Inc.
815 Church Street
Honesdale, Pennsylvania 18431

*For Chuck, who said something to the effect of
"Sure, go ahead and give up a predictable salary
to follow your writing dreams."*

Every writer should be so blessed!

Contents

PROLOGUE

If you ask folks around here what they remember about the
year 1944,

A child might say, "That was the year my daddy went off
to fight Hitler."

A mother might look off towards Bakers Mountain and
whisper that polio snatched up one of her young'uns.

And the *Hickory Daily Record* will say that my hometown
gave birth to a miracle.

If anyone knows about them things, it's me, Ann Fay
Honeycutt, for sure.

But if you ask me what I remember,

I will say it was the year I put on overalls and become the
"man of the house."

It was the summer that wisteria turned enemy on me and
I made best friends with a colored girl.

It was the fall when Franklin D. Roosevelt was elected to
his fourth term in office.

I will say it was the time in my life when I learned that
all of us is fragile as a mimosa blossom.

But I also learned that it mostly hurts at first …

1

The War Hits Home
January 1944

My family huddled together on the railroad platform, but we wasn't huddling to get out of the January wind. We was all trying to stay close to Daddy—like that would keep him home somehow.

At the other end of the platform, under a sign that said COLOREDS, a Negro family was doing the same thing. That's when it hit me how much colored people was just like us.

Daddy took my chin and made me look right at him. "I expect you to be the man of the house while I'm gone," he said. He handed me a pair of blue overalls. "You been wanting to wear britches ever since you first climbed that apple tree. I reckon this is your chance."

Daddy run his finger over the Old Hickory label on the front of them overalls. "See, they was made right here in Hickory, North Carolina."

I knew Daddy would expect me to act like a lady if he was staying home. When I turned thirteen, he started telling me it was time to learn some things from my momma and quit tagging after him all the time. Now, he was telling me to wear britches—which should've made me happy. But wearing britches so I could take the place of my daddy wasn't the same as wearing them so I could climb trees.

I knew I had to do my part for the war. But was this my part, sending Daddy off to fight while I planted the peas?

"Don't look so downhearted," Daddy said. "Your momma always said I spit you right out of my mouth. So you might as well go ahead and take my place for a while."

I took a long look at my daddy with his dimpled chin and his black hair and blue eyes. I soaked up the look of him tall and solid under his new uniform.

I knew I looked just like him. And ever since I could walk, I had chased after him like a train following a railroad track. It didn't matter if he was cutting a hickory branch to make a handle for his shovel or planing a board for a night-stand for Momma, I was right there picking up the curly wood shavings and poking them in his ears.

Daddy always said he had to go hide in the johnny house if he wanted to get a minute without me.

And now, here I was sending him off to fight Hitler.

I threw my arms around him and sucked in the smell of his cigarettes and hair tonic. I hung on tight and felt his heart beating in my chest. Or was it my heart?

After he tore himself away, he picked up my six-year-old sisters, Ida and Ellie, one at a time. He rubbed noses with the twins like he done every morning when he went to work, and said like always, "Now don't you be growing up while I'm gone."

If it was an ordinary day, they would've teased him back. *Just watch. We're gonna get big when you ain't looking.*

But today they didn't have the heart for Daddy's games. And I didn't blame them. Daddy was going off to fight the meanest man in the world, and we knew good and well that we might all have to grow up without him.

Then Daddy picked up my four-year-old brother. "Why

did you give them overalls to Ann Fay?" asked Bobby. "I thought I was gonna be the man of the house."

"Bobby," said Daddy, "you're the only man child I got, but you're just a little man. I expect you to help Momma and Ann Fay, but you gotta take some time to play ever' day."

Daddy ruffled Bobby's brown curls and added, "Now, that's my opinion and it's worth two cents." And just like that, he reached in his pocket and pulled out two pennies. He put one in each of Bobby's chubby hands.

Bobby didn't say nothing about no overalls after that.

Then Daddy put his hands so tender around Momma's head and buried his face in her shiny brown hair like he was sucking in all her smells. He whispered her name and that's all he said. "Myrtle." Like just saying her name would tell her everything else in his heart. She laid her head up against his chest and fingered the muscles in his arms. I thought how I knew the exact feel of his muscles under her fingers. And I knew the ache in her heart too.

Bobby was hanging on to both their legs. Ida and Ellie hugged each other and cried. All of a sudden my family seemed so broke apart. I wanted in the worst way to squeeze us all in Daddy's truck and let him drive us out into the country.

But just then the conductor blew his whistle and called, "All aboard!"

"Oh, Leroy," my momma said. Her voice cracked, and I felt a stab of pain in my throat. Daddy squeezed her one more time and let her go real slow, in a way that seemed like he was really hanging on to her. I think I seen tears in his eyes, but he turned quick and almost run to that train. I looked for him to wave out a window, but he never did, so I knew for sure he was crying.

Down at the other end of the platform, I seen that colored daddy in his uniform getting on the train too.

I tell you what—the sight of them two daddies, the colored daddy and my white one, leaving their women and children at the exact same time, was like the beginning of a journey for me. I didn't go anywhere, really. But I was never in the same place after that either.

The train let off a last big puff of steam and wailed out of the station. Bobby started up howling right along with it. Momma held her hand over his mouth and said, "Hush, now, sugar. Daddy will be back before you know it."

About that time a man started toward us. He was dressed in a black suit with a hat to match, and he had the kindest eyes, which put me in mind of Daddy. The man put his hand in his pocket, and the next thing I knew, he was prying my brother's fist open and putting a nickel in his wet little hand with his wet little pennies. "There now," he said. "I bet if you buy yourself a root beer, you'll feel better in no time."

Well, I reckon Bobby hadn't ever had a whole dope to himself. He swiped his fat wet cheeks with the back of his fists and gulped back his tears and didn't say a word.

Ida whined, "How come Bobby's getting all the money?"

Ellie echoed right after her, "Yeah, how come?"

The man laughed and pulled three more nickels out of his pocket. He started handing them to us girls.

But Momma wasn't used to taking money from strangers. "Sir," she said, "my girls didn't mean to beg."

"Of course they didn't," said the man. "But I want to give it. There's a war on and we all have to share." Then he pulled a five-dollar bill out of his pocket. "While you're at the store, pick up some meat for your supper tonight. The ration board says we can buy pork again. I hope you have some ration coupons."

I reckon the man saw that Momma could use the money. But I didn't think she'd take it. She shook her head and said, "I do have coupons. But I can't take your money."

The man laughed softly. "For these little ones, you can. I have a child too," he said, "so I know how you love them." He shook the bill gently and said, "I can't serve in the war, but I like to support those who can."

Momma must've liked his argument, because she took the five dollars. "I don't know how to thank you," she said.

The man winked at me and patted the twins' blond curls before he walked away.

Then we walked to the parking lot, where our neighbor, Junior Bledsoe, was waiting for us in Daddy's truck. Junior is seventeen years old. He's the man of his house too, ever since his daddy's heart give out a few years ago.

Junior and his momma don't have a car or truck, and my momma don't have a driver's license. So Daddy give his pickup to Junior to use while he's gone—as long as Junior helps look after us. Which Junior would do anyhow, on account of that's just how he is. He's got a big heart, for one thing. Not to mention, he dearly loves being in charge.

When we was driving away from the train station, we seen the man that give Momma the money. That's when I knew why he couldn't serve in the war. And why he got that softness in his voice when he talked about his child.

Him and his wife was pushing a wheelchair with a girl in it. She must have been about the same age as Ida and Ellie. She had braces on both legs, which was real skinny, and I knew the minute I seen her what was wrong.

"Oh, my Lord," I said. "His little girl has got infantile paralysis."

"What's that?" asked Ellie.

"Polio," said Junior. "That's what President Roosevelt had."

I thought how Daddy had told me if Franklin Roosevelt could be crippled and still get himself elected president, then I could handle any hard thing that got thrown at me.

Since Daddy said it, I knew it was true. But with him gone, I wasn't feeling so sure. And seeing that girl with polio put another sadness all over me.

We stopped at the Fresh Air Market and bought a whole dope each. Momma bought one for Junior too, and she give us each a dime of that man's money to put in a little box on the counter. The box had a label that said MARCH OF DIMES. The dimes would go to the president so he could help other people with polio.

"Some people can't even breathe when they get polio," said Junior. "They have to lay in an iron lung with nothing but their head sticking out. It's like a big barrel that does the breathing for them."

Sometimes I wished Junior Bledsoe didn't feel so obligated to tell everything he knows. You'd think at a time like this he could see we was in need of hearing something more cheerful.

Going home just made me feel worse. The first thing I seen was the flag hanging in the front window. It had a blue star on it to show that this was a soldier's house. But I couldn't bear to look at it just then, so I went around to the back porch.

I sat on the cold concrete step rocking myself and praying Daddy would walk out of the johnny house any minute. I

BLUE

told myself maybe he didn't really go to the war. Maybe he just needed a break from me.

I heard a little rattle like the sound of the latch lifting on the outhouse. But it was just a family of seedpods, hanging left over and lonely on the mimosa tree. When the wind blew, they made a sad, clattery sound.

I looked past the mimosa to the pines all covered in wisteria vines, and even that vine, which I dearly love, made me sad for Daddy.

Wisteria is the only thing me and Daddy ever argue about. I say the flower is purple and he says it's blue. I tell him I don't see how anyone can hate a flower that's so beautiful and smells so sweet. Daddy says he don't understand how anyone could love a vine that wraps itself around every limb on a tree like it wants to choke the life out of it.

Last summer he declared war on the wisteria on account of it was making its way toward our garden. First he cut every single wisteria vine back about ten feet, and then he dug a ditch between it and the garden. "There," he said. "I dare that menace to come across my ditch."

"If you destroy Wisteria Mansion, me and Peggy Sue are gonna be mad," I said.

Peggy Sue is my best friend. When we was nine years old, Daddy helped us clear a big space under the pine trees out behind the garden. We made us a mansion with different rooms. It has got to be the most beautiful spot in the world, with the sunlight making lacy shadows on the brown pine-needle floor. The walls are all green from the pines and wisteria. Except for a few weeks in April—then they're full of purple blossoms that hang like bunches of grapes and smell so sweet it nearly knocks you over.

When Daddy declared war on the wisteria, I was afraid

he would kill it all off. But he said he couldn't kill it if he tried.

"Ann Fay," he said, "that vine is just like you. It's mighty pretty, but it's also determined. It would take a powerful strong enemy to destroy either one of you."

I wanted to believe him. But now that Daddy was off to fight a real war, I felt destroyed already.

2

Victory Garden
March 1944

Daddy would've planted the peas in February, and I had every intention of doing the same. But it was practically the middle of March before I got around to it.

I was aggravated with Junior Bledsoe for showing up right when me and Peggy Sue was fixing to run Daddy's tiller. There he was, dragging it out of the shed just like it belonged to him.

"Junior, who said you could take over my garden? I should never've told you I was planting peas today," I said.

Junior had a smudge of black grease across his forehead, and his hair was all messed up. He flapped an oily rag in my direction. "Oh, stop it, Ann Fay. This is a man's job and you know it."

"And Daddy told me I'm the man of the house while he's gone."

"Uh-huh. But he asked me to do the heavy work." Junior took the oil plug out and looked inside.

"Yeah, well, lots of women are doing men's work now that the men are gone. If they got women building battleships, I'm sure I can run a garden tiller. We been planning this all week. Right, Peggy Sue?"

I looked to my best friend, thinking she'd help me out. But she was sitting on the back porch steps twirling her blond hair around a finger, dreaming about something besides working in the garden.

Junior pulled on the starter rope. Nothing happened. "See there?" he said. "It ain't that easy."

"Come on," said Peggy Sue. "Let the man have the job." She tugged on my arm, and I knew she wanted to go off somewhere and play.

One thing about Peggy Sue is, she's not used to working like I am. Her momma has a colored maid doing the housework. Her daddy owns a hosiery mill, so he makes lots of money. And he don't have to go to war. He gets to stay home and run his business because he sells socks to the government for the soldiers overseas.

Peggy Sue was happy to let Junior take my garden job. She grabbed my hand and started running. So I went along with her. We crossed the garden spot and jumped over Daddy's ditch, the one he made to keep the wisteria out.

But in our minds it wasn't a ditch anymore—it was a deep ravine with serpents and giant spiders spilling over the top. And we didn't jump over it—we closed our eyes, held hands, and *flew* over it. All of a sudden we was in a beautiful forest, the home of Wisteria Mansion. It was a sparkly, magical place where bad things could never happen.

Of course, here in the middle of March, the wisteria vines was bare as barbed wire. But in just a few weeks we'd be surrounded by purple blossoms. Then the leaves would be popping out right behind them, making the walls around the mansion thicker and even more secret.

Me and Peggy Sue sat on our favorite rock and dreamed about summer days—wading in the creek that ran nearby and eating tomato sandwiches in the dining room of our mansion.

BLUE

After a while I got up and peeked through a break in the pine trees. Back at the house, Momma was taking clothes off the wash line and Junior was running that tiller through the garden. And I seen Pete, our one-eyed black mutt, following along behind, sniffing in the dirt.

"Come on," I said. And this time I jerked Peggy Sue up and started running. Now that Junior had a row of soil broke up, I had to plant them peas. They was calling for rain and my daddy would be proud of me for getting the peas planted just in time.

Junior asked did I want to try running the tiller. "No," I said. "You wanted to do it. Now do it." The sun was about to slip over the back side of Bakers Mountain, so I needed Junior's help. Even if I did hate to admit it.

I got two hoes out of the shed and handed one to Peggy Sue. "Here," I said. "We got to get them peas in before dark. After that, we'll go to Junior's house and listen to the radio."

We dragged the edges of the hoes in the dirt to make a furrow. The smell of that fresh-turned dirt put me in mind of Daddy. It made me want to plant the best garden in America—and not just because everyone else was planting Victory gardens to help the war effort. I wanted to do it on account of them overalls.

I showed Ida and Ellie how to drop a seed every couple of inches, and I told Bobby to push a little dirt overtop of them.

"But Daddy said I should play ever' day," argued Bobby.

That boy was smack good at getting out of work. When his brown eyes filled up with tears I usually give in to him. But today I seen how he was covered with dirt on all sides from rolling in the garden with Pete. So I said, "You played your share for this day. Now, get to work."

He covered a few seeds, but next thing I knew, he was

spinning himself dizzy on the tire swing and trying to walk. "Look," he said. "I'm drunk."

Then Ellie and Ida wanted their turns on the swing. They wouldn't none of them listen to me when I hollered for them to get back to work.

I finally give up and took a break in the johnny house. While I was in there I thought about the letter we had got from Daddy that week. I had read it so many times I knew it by heart.

Dear family,

How's everything on the home front? I hope you children are helping Momma. Whatever she tells you to do, I want you to listen. No complaining! We all have to do our part to win this war. You do your part there and I do my part here.

Of course I can't tell you anything about where I am or what mission we're working on. But it ain't nothing like home—I can tell you that much. If I was home, I'd be checking the garden every morning to see if the peas had sprouted. Here, there ain't a green leaf in sight. Nothing but bare trees and snow. It's miserable cold.

If you get a chance, please send cigarettes. Right now I can get them from the army. But I don't know how long it will last.

Myrtle, I pray for you and the children every day. I'll be home before you know it.

All my love,

Daddy

I prayed for Daddy every night when I went to bed. I prayed he would come home alive and I would do him proud while he was gone. But to tell the truth—helping Momma with all the work Daddy always done ... well, it was a lot more than I knew how to do sometimes.

While I sat in the outhouse, I heard Daddy talking in my head. He was saying, "If Roosevelt could get himself elected president, then you can handle anything life throws your way."

Well, I didn't think it was right for me to have to play Daddy to them kids, but I knew I didn't have a choice. So I thought about what Daddy would do and I knew he would make a game out of working.

I went outside and hollered at them young'uns, "First one in the garden gets to pick the bedtime story."

You should've seen them racing to the garden when I said that.

By the time Junior was done tilling, the garden was the same size as Daddy always made it—big enough to set our house inside. The peas took up only a small part. I still had to plant a whole bunch of stuff. The hardest part would be keeping them young'uns working.

But Daddy was counting on me. I decided that if I had to, I'd work them kids till we all dropped.

3

Wisteria Mansion
April 1944

Me and Peggy Sue laid on the soft pine-needle floor of Wisteria Mansion, ignoring my sisters. They'd been in the back yard calling my name for fifteen minutes. But I wasn't about to answer them. This was one place we could go to get away from the girls and Bobby. So Peggy and me agreed a long time ago not to show it to anyone unless we asked each other first.

Wisteria Mansion was where we always run to when we wanted to feel better. Right now was one of those times.

Peggy's eyes was red from crying. "I can't believe Lottie Scronce's other boy was killed," she said.

Lottie is a woman who goes to our church. All the children love her because she keeps candy in her pocketbook and hands it out every Sunday.

I turned over on my back and sucked in the sweet smell of wisteria, trying to chase away the bad feeling in my tummy. "Two boys in one family lost to the war," I said. "It don't seem fair. Nothing about this war is fair."

"I know what you're thinking," said Peggy Sue. "But your daddy is going to come home safe and sound. I just know he is."

She didn't know any such thing. But as my best friend she had to make promises she couldn't keep. It was her job to make me feel better.

"I know," I said. "I know he'll come home."

But of course I didn't know. I stared up through the ceiling of our mansion to the blue sky, wishing I could see God. I'd ask Him a thing or two about this war.

Right now the mansion was as beautiful as it would ever get. A warm breeze made the sunlight and shadows do a dance that wouldn't stop. You could see it sparkling on every pine tree. The wisteria blossoms hung down through the branches of the pines so that the ceiling and the walls were covered over in purple glory.

Or blue, if you asked my daddy.

The smell of it was so sweet it made my throat ache. I ached for the old days when Daddy and I argued over whether that smell was purple or blue. I ached over the meanness of war. I knew if I could just stay here and the blossoms didn't die, I could forget about the war.

But the blossoms never lasted long enough. Last week, me and Peggy Sue took some wisteria flowers and pressed them between the pages of our history books so we could take the sweetness to school with us.

I even sent a pressed blossom in a letter to Daddy. As best I can remember, this is what I wrote:

Dear Daddy,

As you can see, your war didn't kill the wisteria. Only slowed it down, I reckon. I thought if I sent you a little bit of home, it would cheer you up. I hope it still smells sweet when you get this. The flowers are purpler than ever!

We got the peas in the ground with Junior's help. They're up about two inches and the rains have been coming right along. The potatoes are in too. We got a good start on the garden, although it would be way better if you was here to help.

I hope you're safe. I pray for you every night and during the day too. I love you better than molasses cookies. (Momma is making you some to put in this package.)
      Love,
            Ann Fay

I hoped that getting a purplish blue flower from home in the middle of the war would change the way Daddy felt about that pesky vine. But mostly I hoped Peggy Sue was right about Daddy coming home safe and sound.

Whenever the breeze picked up, little purple petals rained down on me and Peggy Sue. They shimmered all the way down, and I wondered how in the world God could have saved anything prettier just for heaven.

4

Polio!
June 1944

By the middle of June the garden was full of vegetable plants. It had some weeds too, but still, I thought my daddy would be proud.

He wrote every couple of weeks. We got a letter the third week of June.

Dear family,

My eyes are sore for the sight of women and children. Especially my woman and my children. And the blue sky and red clay of Carolina would be a wondrous sight too.

I know you hear on the radio what's going on in the war. We're making progress in our mission, but the Germans won't stop fighting even when they're licked. So I may be here longer than we thought. War is terrible.

I'm glad to hear the peas done good. Ann Fay, you do me proud the way you're filling those overalls.

Bobby, I have your drawings in my pack, and I take them out and look at them whenever I get a minute. It makes me feel almost like I'm home.

Ida and Ellie, Momma says you done good in school. I'm right proud of every one of you.

All my love,
    Daddy

We wrote Daddy every week, and every so often we sent him a package with comforts like soap and chewing gum and cigarettes.

Whenever we sent one of them packages, Bobby dumped his box of crayons out on the kitchen table. He drew pictures of tigers and other wild animals on his drawing tablet. We always asked Bobby what message he wanted us to write on his pictures. Every time, he said the same thing. "Tell Daddy, 'Good night, sleep tight, don't let the bedbugs bite.'"

I kept wondering if Daddy had took part in D-Day. That was the day—June 6—when our boys landed on the beaches of France and started taking that country back from the big bully, Hitler. I wondered if they would push into Germany next.

President Roosevelt come on the radio twice in June to tell us what was going on. The first time, he told how our boys and the other Allied soldiers took Rome away from the Germans. A week later, he come on to announce a new war-loan drive. That's where ordinary Americans like me can loan money to the government for building ships and airplanes and whatever else our soldiers need. And he reminded us of all the good our money done, helping our soldiers drive back the Germans and the Japanese from all those places they had took over.

Talk of the war was everywhere. Even at church on Sundays. The preacher always said a prayer for the soldiers. There was eleven men from our church fighting in the war, not counting Lottie Scronce's two boys that had already been killed.

Lottie cried all the way through every church service, but she kept coming. And every week she snapped open her big black pocketbook and pulled out mints for all the little children. She'd been doing that for as long as I could remember.

After I'd sweated in the garden all week, going to church was almost as good as going to the movies with Peggy Sue. Somehow it helped me get through another week just to hear Reverend Price say my daddy's name in a prayer.

But one Sunday in the middle of June, the reverend stopped us at the church door. His red hair was damp around the edges. Little rivers of sweat was running past his ears, and his white shirt had wet circles under the arms.

"I'm sorry, Mrs. Honeycutt," he said. "I guess you hadn't heard. We've canceled Sunday school."

Momma stopped dead in her tracks. "No, I hadn't heard."

"There are twelve cases of polio in Catawba County right now. I thought you would have read it in the paper or heard it on the radio."

"Oh my dear," said Momma. She grabbed Bobby's hand and pulled him up against her.

The reason Momma didn't know is, we was so busy in the garden and just trying to keep up. We hadn't been to Junior's house to listen to the radio, except two times to hear the president's speeches. And we don't get the paper either. Sometimes we read our neighbors' newspaper—the Hinkle sisters' copy—when they're done with it.

"All public meetings are closed to children twelve and under," said Reverend Price.

I felt sweat running down the inside of my dress.

"And playgrounds too," said the preacher. "And theaters and swimming pools."

While he stood there and listed all the things we couldn't do, I had a feeling like every good thing in my life was being taken away.

"Hopefully this will all blow over," said Reverend Price. "Be sure to listen to WHKY today. At twelve forty-five, Dr. Whims, the county health officer, will make an announcement about polio."

Right away Bessie Bledsoe invited us to listen at their house. But I wasn't ready to turn around and leave. I was counting on seeing my friends. So I asked Momma could Peggy Sue come to my house to play.

Momma fluffed the back of my hair a little to let the breeze cool my neck. "Yes, honey," she said. "Lord knows you deserve it."

Me and Peggy Sue run to her mother, who was standing with some other women under a shade tree in the churchyard. She was fanning herself with one of them church fans put out by a funeral home. It had a picture of Jesus praying in the garden, sweating drops of blood.

"Please let her come, Mrs. Rhinehart," I begged. "We want to wade in the creek." I flapped my hands in front of my face, like I would just die if we couldn't get in the water.

Mrs. Rhinehart reached in her black pocketbook and pulled out a cotton handkerchief with blue flowers embroidered on the corner. She used it to dab beads of sweat off the space between her nose and her upper lip. She got bright red lipstick on the handkerchief when she done that.

"It's just the children under twelve that are banned," she said. "The two of you can stay for church. Afterwards you could come to our house and get wet with the water hose. My husband can take you home this afternoon."

But Peggy Sue wanted to come to my house, and that girl has got herself a knack for getting what she wants. So we climbed in the back of Daddy's pickup with Ida and Ellie.

BLUE

Junior Bledsoe drove the truck, and his momma and mine sat up front with Bobby.

At Junior's house we sat on the grass under a shade tree, and Bessie served us all iced tea and milk with peanut butter crackers. Bessie and Momma sat on rocking chairs on the porch.

"Have mercy," Bessie panted. "It sure is hot." She pulled up her apron and flapped it in her face to create a little wind. Bessie is a big woman, so it don't take much to heat her up.

And we was all sweating today—even in the shade.

Ida and Ellie and Bobby played with Junior's hound dogs, and Junior entertained them at the same time, trying to catch the flies buzzing around his head.

Me and Peggy Sue got tired of Junior showing off. So we went and sat on the steps when Momma and Bessie started talking about polio.

"My cousin's child had it," said Bessie. "One day she was frolicking like a baby goat and the next she was flat on her back. Poor baby hasn't walked since."

Momma shivered and I seen the goose bumps come up on her arms, even in that heat.

"It's just awful how it paralyzes little children," said Bessie.

Momma nodded. "And not just children. Take our president—a full-grown man when he got it. You have to wonder how a man like that gets polio."

"My cousin has no idea how little Winnie got it," said Bessie. "As far as any of them can remember, she never got close to anyone with polio."

Of course, Junior being Junior, he had to get his two cents' worth in. He come over to the porch. "Even the doctors don't know how polio gets passed around," he said.

I rolled my eyes and said, "Oh boy, here we go." Thinking he'd take a hint and go back to catching flies.

But he kept right on. "Did you hear about that woman in Virginia that kept her children in the house all last summer just because someone across town came down with polio?"

Listening to them mothers worrying about polio was making me feel jittery enough without Junior piling on more bad news. "Junior Bledsoe," I said, "how would you know what some woman in Virginia did once upon a time?"

"Well, I do listen to the radio once in a while, Ann Fay."

"Well then, I reckon that makes you the polio expert, don't it?"

"Now, you two," said Momma. "We're all a little nervous, but that's no reason to go starting up a fight. We need to stick together in times like this."

At twelve forty-five we went inside to hear the radio announcement. We all sat at the edge of our seats because we didn't want to miss a word Dr. Whims said.

He declared that we had an epidemic, on account of so many cases of infantile paralysis in the state—and especially in our county. He said, "Of ten cases, four went swimming or wading and two were near water or fishing within a few days before the onset of the disease. It is advisable that adults as well as children refrain from going swimming while the epidemic is in progress."

You should've heard us groan when he said that. Bessie's thermometer was pushing a hundred degrees and the man was telling us we couldn't go in the creek.

"Holy mackerel!" Ida wailed.

"We're gonna die," moaned Ellie.

Dr. Whims talked about screen doors and how we should keep flies out of the house because they might spread the disease.

"I see one," said Bobby. He run to the screen door and tried to catch it.

"I don't see why we can't go swimming," whined Ida.

"Yeah," said Ellie. "That man is not our daddy."

Momma said, "No, but the health officer is responsible for the whole county. I'm sure he knows what he's doing."

"Momma," I said, "can't me and Peggy Sue go wading one last time?"

Momma shook her head. "I could never forgive myself if you came down with polio."

We walked home. It was only about a half-mile, but we dripped sweat the whole way. Me and Peggy Sue lagged behind the rest. "We'll go down to the creek when your momma and the young'uns are taking their Sunday afternoon naps," said Peggy Sue. "Let's dam up the water with rocks and make a deep place to sit in."

But just then we heard a car coming behind us. When we turned around, Peggy Sue said, "What's my daddy doing here?" We stopped and waited for his shiny black car to stop beside us.

Mr. Rhinehart tipped his black hat to my momma. "Hello, Mrs. Honeycutt. Can I give you all a ride home?"

Momma laughed and pointed to our mailbox, which wasn't a stone's throw away. "Now, if you had come just fifteen minutes sooner," she said.

Mr. Rhinehart laughed too. "Well, I wish I had. Brenda sent me to get Peggy Sue. I guess you heard the radio announcement about swimming. She said the girls were planning to play in the creek."

"Yes. But I won't let them. Don't worry about that."

"Please, Daddy, please let me stay," begged Peggy Sue. "I'll stay out of the creek. I promise."

But I reckon her daddy knew better than to believe that. He shook his head. "Your mother's expecting you to come home," he said. "We'd better not disappoint her."

"But Daddy ..."

Momma nudged Peggy in the back. "Go on, child," she said. "You can come another day. Just as soon as this passes."

Peggy was so mad she climbed in the back seat and left her daddy up front all by himself. He turned the car around in our lane and tipped his hat again when he passed us. Peggy rolled her eyes and pouted when they went by.

The day was ruined for sure and it looked like the whole entire summer was too. I reckon me and Peggy Sue both knew it could be a long time before we saw each other again.

5

Bobby
June 1944

Twice that week Momma sent me to the Hinkle sisters' house to borrow newspapers. She wanted to keep up on the polio news.

Tuesday's paper said an eight-year-old boy had died of polio. And it told how there were nineteen cases in the county. Seven more just since Sunday!

In Thursday's paper we read that a camp in Hickory was going to become an emergency hospital for polio victims. We also read that three doctors from Yale University had come to Hickory to investigate our epidemic. Imagine that!

The next Tuesday, Bobby come down with a cold, which scared Momma half to death. He sneezed and she stopped sweeping the front porch. She pulled Daddy's big red hanky from her apron pocket and held it to Bobby's nose. "Blow, honey," she said. Then she stuffed the hanky in Bobby's pocket, sat down on a rocking chair, and pulled him onto her lap.

She rested her chin on Bobby's head and I seen again how much that boy looked just like her. They had the same shiny brown curls and deep red lips. And both had brown eyes that squinted nearly shut when they laughed. But neither one of them was laughing now.

"I can't recall him being around anyone who had a

cold," Momma said. Her rocking chair was making a fast, irritating sound on the wood porch floor, and it was making me edgy.

I knew exactly what she was thinking. "Stop worrying, Momma," I said. "A cold ain't the same thing as polio. And he ain't been around nobody that has polio neither. So you can just put that outta your mind."

Momma sighed. "I know," she said. She used her toe to slow that rocking chair down. "You're right, of course."

Bobby curled up on Momma's lap and snuggled into her like he was trying to crawl inside her heart. But Bobby had been in Momma's heart since before he was born. I can still remember how she'd walk around hugging her big tummy with her hands and getting so lost in her happy thoughts that she'd forget which scrubbing job she was working on. It seemed like she knew she was finally getting herself a man child.

But this week, what with taking care of Bobby, Momma didn't hardly scrub a thing. She smeared vapor rub on his chest and kept it covered with a warm, wet cloth. She made him stay in bed for two days, where she sung to him and told him Bible stories and played with him and his wooden farm animals.

And it seemed like Bobby's cold went away in no time. Thursday morning when I woke up, he was outside spinning the tire swing with Pete inside—and falling down laughing when Pete couldn't walk straight afterwards.

"Bobby looks like he's all better," I said to Momma while I ate my gravy biscuit. She was pouring soap powders into the dishpan and fixing to scrub down the kitchen, but I could hear her sigh of relief all the way across the room.

"Yeah, he's back to pestering that dog again, so I reckon he'll be fine," she said.

"Good," I said. "Then he can help us bring in the potatoes."

After breakfast, I give Ida, Ellie, and Bobby a warning. "We're turning into farmers in five minutes," I said. "And I want you to be in the garden with a bushel basket in your hand."

Ida was the first to whine. "I don't want to work in the garden. Me and Ellie was going to play paper dolls."

"Yeah," whined Ellie.

"No," I said. "Not until we get this done. These potatoes are gonna rot if we don't get them out of the ground. And tomorrow we pick blackberries. Then we're gonna go buy sugar because the ration board said we can get our share for canning." I figured if I mentioned a trip to town they might work harder.

"I can't work," said Bobby. "I'm sick." He was carrying Pete wrapped up like a baby in his blue striped blanket.

"You don't look sick to me," I said.

"Pete's sick," said Bobby. "He's blind in one eye and his legs is aching."

"Pete's been blind in one eye ever since he tangled with that groundhog last year," I said. "And if his legs is sore, then he don't have to work. But you do. Bring the wagon when you come."

Bobby was the first to show up in the garden. He was pulling the wagon and Pete was inside on Bobby's blanket. That dog was getting plumb spoiled. Bobby hadn't let him out of his sight since Daddy went off to war.

I wished a little old dog could take Daddy's place for *me*.

I had to holler for the girls to get out to the garden, and

by then I had a whole row of potatoes dug and waiting to be put in baskets. Bobby didn't do a thing but mess with that dog until the girls got there.

Ida showed up with a bushel basket over her head so she couldn't half see where she was going. She had another basket in her hand. Ellie was empty-handed.

I made the young'uns put the potatoes in the baskets. Then we put the baskets in the wagon and pulled it to the dirt cellar under the back of the house.

When the potatoes was unloaded, Bobby put Pete in the wagon and climbed in with him. "Giddyup, horse," he said. "Me and Pete wants a ride."

So I pulled the two of them back to the garden. But I didn't get much work out of him after that first trip. He whined and fussed and said he hurt all over.

The girls fussed too, and Ida said I was meaner than the devil himself.

"Listen here!" I yelled. "I reckon you think I'm doing this for fun. Well, I'm not! I'm doing it on account of there's a war on and Daddy can't be here to look after his family. So stop bellyaching and do your part."

The girls started picking up potatoes, but Bobby was collecting fluffy pink mimosa blossoms from the tree by the edge of the garden. "I'm sick," he said when I called him back to the garden. He tickled Pete's nose with a mimosa flower. Pete sneezed and Bobby giggled. "See?" he said. "Me and Pete has got a cold."

If Daddy was there, he would've found a way to make working fun. But I was hot and had blisters on my hands, so I was irritable.

"Bobby Leroy Honeycutt, if you don't get to work, I'm gonna write Daddy a letter. And I'll say a lot more than

'Good night, sleep tight, don't let the bedbugs bite.' I'll tell him you're a spoiled little brat that won't do nothing but play with the dog."

Bobby started crying then, but he got up and put a few potatoes in a basket. It didn't last long. By the time the next load of potatoes was ready, he was back sitting in the dirt and scooping dry dust over Pete's tail and watching it fly around when Pete wagged it off. I didn't even bother calling him to help. He was way more trouble than he was worth.

After all, he was only four years old, and the last thing Daddy told him was to play some every day. So I guessed I shouldn't be so hard on him, even if picking up potatoes wasn't really that much work.

By the time we got halfway to the cellar, Bobby was screaming for us to come back and get him. I just kept right on pulling that wagon.

Ida stopped.

"Don't you dare go after him," I said. "Bobby's got two good legs the same as the rest of us." But she didn't pay me no mind.

Of course, Ellie followed right after her. Soon they was all three screaming. Momma come out on the porch to see what all the clamor was about, so I let her take over while I laid the potatoes out in the root cellar. Next thing I knew, Momma was hollering too.

I run down there to see what was the matter. Momma was trying to get Bobby to stand up. But his legs was just crumpling underneath him and his arms was floppy too. I didn't need no doctor to tell me what was wrong.

Momma picked Bobby up and took him inside, and the three of us girls was right behind her. She turned to me and said, "Jump on the bicycle and go get Junior to bring the truck. He's got to take us to the emergency hospital."

I pedaled that bicycle fast as I could, and my heart was bumpier than that dirt road. All I could think of was how mean I was, making Bobby work when he was really sick.

But he didn't seem sick at the beginning. Momma checked his forehead in the morning and he didn't have no fever. And he was giggling and playing and he didn't seem sick at all. But still, I knew it was my fault for yelling at him like that. And using that threat about Daddy to shame him into working when he didn't feel up to it.

I preached myself a sermon all the way to Junior's.

When I got there, Junior was laying under the truck in the driveway. Wrenches and car parts was scattered on the ground by his legs. I started yelling the minute I seen him. "Junior, I need you right this minute! And the truck too. You got to take Bobby to the doctor's."

Junior come sliding out from under the truck and said, "What's the matter? Can it wait? I got to put this thing back together or we ain't going nowhere."

"Junior Bledsoe, why are you taking Daddy's truck apart? He said you could use it so you could take Momma places— not take it apart." I started beating on his chest.

"Whoa, girl! What has got into you?" Junior grabbed my hands and held me back from him.

"Bobby's got polio," I said. "He has to get to the emergency hospital in Hickory."

"Oh, Lordy," said Junior. "This truck ain't going nowhere for a while. We better see if the Hinkle sisters can take you." He run and got his bicycle then. I could hardly keep up with him going up the dirt road to the Hinkles'.

I knew we was in trouble the minute we got there

because the Hinkle sisters' car was not in the garage behind their brick house. "They're not home," I said.

I just knew Bobby was going to die while we rode around looking for someone to take him to the hospital.

"Then we'll use their telephone," said Junior.

We hurried to the back door and went inside. "Anybody home?" yelled Junior as he run through the kitchen. The Hinkle sisters' kitchen was just like always. The counter-tops and stove was spotless. The plants on the windowsill was cheerful. Everything was in its place and quiet as midnight.

We kept going into the dining room. Junior grabbed the heavy black telephone off the little table so fast the cord drug the white lace doily onto the floor. I sunk into the chair beside the telephone table.

Junior dialed the operator. "I need Dr. Johnson," he said.

A clock on the wall tick-tick-ticked, bragging on how much precious time was slipping by.

Finally Junior handed me the telephone. A lady asked how could she help me. I told her about Bobby collapsing in the garden. But it seemed like she couldn't understand.

"Slow down, honey," she said.

But I knew we didn't have no time to waste. I told her what happened to Bobby and how we didn't have a car to take him to the doctor's. She put Dr. Johnson on the telephone and I had to tell it all over again. He said he would send an ambulance. I give the receiver to Junior so he could give directions.

I put my head down on the telephone and my tears run down over the numbers on the dial. "He's only four years old," I moaned. "And I made him work even when he said he was sick. Oh, Daddy, I should've let him play."

The next thing I knew, Junior was pushing a glass of water to me. "Here, Ann Fay," he said. "Drink this water and calm down. Everything will be all right."

But I knew he was just saying that to get me through. I knew nothing was ever going to be all right again.

6

Epidemiologists
June 1944

We crowded around Bobby while we waited for the ambulance. He was laying on the couch with his head on Momma's lap, still as a stop sign. Not even his eyes was moving.

"He's dead," wailed Ida.

"No," said Momma. "He's still breathing—and feel how warm he is."

I grabbed ahold of his hand and it was hot. But I was cold—shivering and shaking and my teeth wouldn't stop chattering. It seemed like we was all shivering and huddling up to Bobby like he was a woodstove in the middle of winter. I forgot all about how it was a hot day.

Junior kept walking to the window to look for the ambulance and then coming back to offer us a drink of water. Or to touch Momma on the shoulder like he wanted to take Daddy's place but didn't know how.

And I for sure didn't feel like the man of the house.

Finally we heard a car. Junior run to the window and said, "Somebody's here. But it's sure not an ambulance."

Momma picked Bobby up and carried him out on the porch, and we all followed. Then I seen what Junior meant. It wasn't an ambulance. It was a hearse.

Momma cried, "No! Oh, dear God, no." She turned to go back in the house.

By that time the driver had backed up to the steps and was climbing out of the hearse. "Don't let it scare you, ma'am," he said. "There's a shortage of ambulances, what with the war taking so many and now the epidemic. Sometimes this is the only way we can get a child to the polio hospital. But it can save your boy's life just as good as an ambulance." He opened the doors in the back, and inside was a low bed.

Junior put his hands on Momma's shoulders and turned her around. "It's okay," he said.

The driver come and tried to take Bobby from Momma, but she held on tight. "Ma'am, you can come along with him. Is there anything you want to get, in case you need to stay a few days?"

Momma shook her head and I knew she wasn't thinking straight. If she was, she wouldn't want to be seen in her everyday dress and apron. So I run and got her pocketbook. And I grabbed her nightgown and housecoat from the nail on the back of her bedroom door. Daddy had took our suitcase off to the war, so I pulled the pillowcase off her pillow and stuffed her nightgown in it. And I threw in some underclothes and her Sunday dress and run outside.

When I got there, Momma was kneeling by Bobby in the back of that hearse, hanging on to his limp hands. I threw the pillowcase bundle to her right before the driver closed the door.

It all happened so fast that none of us said goodbye to Bobby. And even though Momma said he wasn't dead, it sure made us feel like he was, him riding away in that hearse like that.

Junior stayed with us the rest of the day and helped us dig the potatoes. I would've let them rot in the ground if he hadn't been there to nag at me. Then he hoed weeds.

I couldn't force myself to cook supper, so I just poured a bowl of corn flakes for everybody. Nobody but Junior had an appetite. He tried to cheer us up by playing a game of pretend.

"Let's pretend we're going to Hollywood," he said.

Hollywood is the last place I'd expect Junior Bledsoe to want to go. But I reckon he thought us girls would like the idea.

"Let's pretend we can see anybody famous that we want to," he said. "Who do you want to see, Ida?"

Ida twirled her spoon through her cereal. "Bobby," she said. "I wanna see Bobby."

"Oh," said Junior. "But what about a movie star? Which movie star do you want to see?"

Ida just stared. "I don't wanna see no movie stars."

"Sure you do," said Junior with an extra helping of cheer in his voice. "Oh, I know—you want to see Shirley Temple, don't you?"

Ida picked up her spoon and held it out in front of her. She turned the spoon sideways and watched as the corn flakes and milk dribbled off and plopped into her bowl.

Junior give up on Ida then and turned to Ellie. "What about you? Let's pretend Shirley Temple is standing there with her head full of curls, cute as anything, right in front of you. What would you say to her?"

Ellie slumped back in her chair and folded her arms. She didn't say a word.

"Well," said Junior, "I see I'm on my own here. Okay then, let's pretend we all go to Hollywood and suddenly, right there in front us, is James Cagney. Now wouldn't *that* be a Yankee Doodle Dandy?"

For some reason Junior is real keen on James Cagney.

And he knew me and Peggy Sue seen him in the movie *Yankee Doodle Dandy*. But Junior was wrong if he thought a movie star could take my mind off of Bobby and what I done to him.

I got up and put my bowl of cereal in the refrigerator. "Let's pretend Bobby's not sick," I said. "Let's pretend you ain't sitting there acting like everything is all hunky-dory dandy. If we pretend, will that make it true?"

Junior dropped his spoon in his bowl and said, "I'm sorry, Ann Fay. I was just trying to help."

"Well, don't," I said. "On account of it ain't working."

I went outside on the back steps and stared at the johnny house, wishing a miracle would step out that door.

Instead, Junior come to the screen door behind me. "I reckon I'll be getting on home," he said. "But I'll be back in the morning."

"Don't worry about us," I said. "We'll be fine." Which was a lie if I ever told one.

Of course, there was no point in telling Junior not to come back. The next morning he was on our front porch, calling my name. I was drawing water from the well and wondering how in the world my momma and Bobby was doing. "I'm out back," I yelled.

He come around the side of the house with a small crock in his hand. "Momma sent you some bread pudding," he said. "She's sorry it's not sweeter, but we're out of sugar till we pick it up at the ration board today. I got the starter fixed, so the truck is ready whenever you are." He handed me the crock and finished cranking the water bucket up out of the well.

I took the bread pudding inside and let the screen door slam behind me. "I don't think I'll go for sugar," I said. "I might not can blackberries after all."

Junior followed me inside and poured the bucket of water into our water crock on the kitchen cabinet. "Don't start talking like that," he said. "According to the papers, this is our last allotment of sugar for canning this year. I'd pick it up for you except you have to be there in person with your ration book. I'll help you pick them berries, but you gotta do your part. You can't just stop living."

"I don't wanna pick blackberries," I said. "I don't wanna can them and I don't wanna buy sugar. I just wanna go to the emergency hospital and see Bobby."

"Well, Ann Fay, I know how you must feel. But according to the radio they got the police over there keeping people away from that hospital. The best thing you can do for Bobby is pick those berries and fix him some blackberry cobbler the minute he comes home. So get your overalls on."

He just had to mention them overalls.

I knew if it wasn't for Junior I would just run off through the woods and stay out of the garden and the blackberry patch too. But there was work to do and I was the man of the house. So I put on my overalls.

Just then I heard a car pull up outside, and both me and Junior went running to see if it was Momma and Bobby back from the hospital. But two women got out of the shiny black car. The tall woman in the plaid dress spoke up. "I'm Dr. Dorothy Horstmann." Then she nodded toward the other woman. "And this is Frances Allen, your public health nurse."

"Hey," I said. "I'm Ann Fay Honeycutt."

"Ann Fay, I'm an epidemiologist from Yale Medical School," Dr. Horstmann said. "I study diseases, especially polio."

"I know," I said. "I seen you in the papers."

"Then you know we work at the emergency hospital," she continued. "We looked in on your brother this morning. He's breathing easily with the help of an iron lung."

An iron lung! All of a sudden I couldn't catch my breath.

I think that Frances Allen woman seen it too. "Oh, don't let the iron lung worry you," she said. "Right now, it's keeping him alive until he can breathe for himself again."

That give me some hope, so I asked, "Is he gonna get better?"

She squeezed my shoulder and said, "He has good doctors, some of the best in the country. Even one of the doctors from the president's Warm Springs polio rehabilitation center is at the hospital."

Dr. Horstmann give me a letter from my momma. She waited while I read it.

Dear Ann Fay,

I just can't leave Bobby here alone. He's too little and he's very sick. I can't get close to him yet, but I can stand outside the door of his ward and wave to him.

The hospital needs my help too. I'm working in the kitchen. I know I can count on you to take care of the girls. And Junior and Bessie will help, too.

Remember the man who gave us money at the train station? He volunteers at the emergency hospital. He invited me to stay with his family as long as I need to. I wouldn't have the gas coupons to go back and forth every day, but he lives nearby. Him and his wife want to help as much as possible because of their little girl, who had polio.

Their phone number is 0577. If I don't come home by Thursday, I want you to go to the Hinkles' around 7:00

in the morning and call me. I'll be free then and I'll tell
you how Bobby is doing. You and the girls say a prayer for
him.

      All my love,
          Momma

Thursday morning! It was just Friday now. How could I wait till Thursday? It almost killed me to think Momma could be gone that long.

Dr. Horstmann didn't give me no time to worry about seeing Momma or Bobby. She told me she and Nurse Allen was going to examine our house and ask lots of questions. They needed to find out how Bobby caught the disease.

I spent the morning answering questions for them strangers. They wanted to know what kind of milk we drunk and where our toilet facilities was. They asked me who Bobby had seen or touched or played with in the last couple of weeks. They went through every room in the house taking notes.

I hadn't washed a single dish since yesterday morning, and the chamber pot hadn't been emptied either. Not only that—one of the girls had left the lid off of the chamber pot and there was flies crawling over it like ants on a jelly biscuit.

I put the lid on quick, hoping those women wouldn't notice. But they did. They even set up a trap to catch them flies. Dr. Horstmann explained to me how the poliovirus had been found on flies and trapping them would help her research.

The twins was both awake by now and hanging on to Junior like he was their daddy.

"Which one of you left the lid off of the chamber pot?" I

asked. I wasn't expecting either one of them to admit to it. I just wanted them women to know we don't make it a habit to live like that.

But how could I make them understand? When your baby brother gets hauled off in a hearse with the most dreaded disease in the country, all on account of you making him work till he dropped, you just can't make yourself do all the things you do any other day.

Before those women inspected our johnny house, I told them, "Don't worry. It's clean. My momma takes disinfectant and a broom to it once a week. She scrubs it top to bottom." I felt bad that these women wasn't getting a true impression of my momma's housekeeping. And I was sure glad Momma wasn't there to see how I had let it go.

As soon as them women was gone, a health officer come and hammered a sign on the front door.

INFANTILE PARALYSIS
IN QUARANTINE

I tell you what's the truth. When I looked at that polio sign next to the blue star flag Momma hung up there for Daddy being a soldier, I felt like I was looking down a double-barrel shotgun—and fixing to get blowed all to pieces.

"How many people live here?" the health officer asked.

"Just me and my two sisters," I said. "Momma went to the hospital with my brother. My daddy's off fighting in the war."

The health officer looked at Junior. "You a neighbor?"

"Yes, sir," said Junior. "You passed right by my house coming in."

"Well," said the man, "I'm afraid you'll have to leave. Only family members are allowed in this house."

Well, I could tell Junior Bledsoe wasn't going to take that sitting down. He stuck his thumbs under the clasps on his overalls and said, "Sir, these girls' momma and daddy didn't have no choice in the matter. But I'll be dad-gummed if I'm going to run off and leave them too."

The officer said, "Well, it's the law. So you really don't have any choice either. I'll drop you off at your house on the way out."

Junior started to argue, but I jumped in. "Aw, go on, Junior," I said. "I can take care of the girls and you know it. What do you think my daddy give me these overalls for? I'm the man of the house now."

I winked at Junior when the man wasn't looking, so he could see I knew him well enough to realize he'd be back—as soon as that man was out of sight.

Before they left, the man turned to me and said, "I can see you're a strong young woman. That's good, because I'm going to ask you to do one of the hardest things you've ever done."

He took my arm and pulled me aside—away from Ida and Ellie—and spoke real low so they couldn't hear what he was saying. "I need you to wash every blanket and towel in the house. And all of your brother's clothes. Scrub the house. Anything your brother touched could have the germs."

The man took a deep breath and lowered his voice even more. "And here's the hard part. Your brother's toys must be destroyed. I want you to burn them. It's the only way to get rid of the germs. It's the only way to protect your little sisters. Understand?"

I think I nodded at him. I guess I agreed. I must have. Because it seems like he patted me on the back and said, "Good, I know you can do it. I'll check back on you tomorrow."

Then him and Junior got in his car and drove off.

When they was gone, I tried to talk myself into burning Bobby's toys. But I didn't get around to it for the rest of the day. There's never a good time to do something like that, especially with two little girls watching your every move. So I started scrubbing down the house and washing all the clothes and towels and sheets, which I didn't nearly get done before Junior come and took us to the ration board for our sugar.

When we was almost there, it hit me and Junior that I wasn't even supposed to go because of the quarantine. But I knew I had to show my own ration stamps, and so far nobody besides us and Junior knew anything about that quarantine sign, so I decided to go in quick and leave quick. I made the girls stay in the car.

While I waited in line for the sugar, I studied the war posters lined up on the wall. They was all about stuff I should be doing to help the war effort—plant Victory gardens, buy war bonds, and give my cooking grease to the butcher so he could give it to the army to make explosives. And that was just the beginning.

It seemed like you couldn't go anywhere without seeing Victory posters. They used to make me feel proud and helpful. I wanted to do what they said because it made me feel like I was helping to win the war. But today, just looking at a picture of a soldier and the words DO THE JOB HE LEFT BEHIND drained the last bit of energy right out of me.

All the way home, I hung on to that sack of sugar like it was my sweet daddy.

7

Bobby's Toys
July 1944

I didn't burn them toys before I went to bed that night. I thought I would do it after Ida and Ellie went to sleep, but I just didn't have the heart for it. So I decided to wait till morning. Maybe in the light of day I could talk myself into it. If not, there was always Junior Bledsoe.

Didn't he promise Daddy he'd do the hard work?

Bobby had a farm set Daddy carved him little by little when he got a chance. He carved a tractor and a whole pile of farm animals. And last Christmas he built a barn to go with them.

I put that farm set and Bobby's stuffed bear, his crayons and drawing pad and his building blocks, in a pasteboard box. I set the box in a corner of the kitchen.

"Don't touch them," I told Ida and Ellie. "On account of the polio germs."

When I finally fell asleep that night, I dreamed I was building a fire in the yard and the whole time I was thinking that it would just kill Bobby if I burned his things. Then in my dream all his toys come marching out of the house and jumped one by one into the flames. The last thing to come out was his crayons and drawing tablet. I knew that tablet was full of Bobby's wild animals on the front and back of every page. So I yelled, "Stop! Don't burn them animals."

But a tiger jumped off a page and screamed at me—and what he screamed was, "Polio germs!" Then he grabbed the tablet in his mouth and jumped into the fire and him and the tablet was both gone.

I woke up then, and I was so scared my heart was racing and I had to get out of bed just to walk the wooziness out of my legs. I sat on a chair at the kitchen table and stared at that box of toys sitting sad and shadowy in the corner. I kept thinking I had already hurt Bobby enough. What would he say when he come home and seen what else I done?

I wished Momma was there to tell me what to do.

But I already knew what she would do. It would break Momma's heart, but she would protect Ida and Ellie from getting polio.

I thought about Daddy and President Roosevelt, and between the two of them making me strong, I grabbed that box of toys quick and went outside to get it over with.

First I made sure the twins was sound asleep. I knew that sooner or later they would miss Bobby's things, but they sure didn't have to see them burn up.

I piled the toys in the yard beside the shed. To get the fire started, I tore up his drawing book and crumbled the pages fast, without looking at them animals. I threw the crayons in and held a match to a page and watched the flame eat it up. Then I sat on the porch steps and watched that fire grow till it sent sparks up into the night sky.

I felt like I was beating my baby brother with a stick.

I decided right then and there I was going to find some way to buy him a new drawing tablet and crayons. I knew if I could save up money for war bonds, which I was doing ever since the war begun, I could sure find some way to buy my brother some toys.

All of a sudden I heard the screen door creak behind me, and there was Ida in her undershirt and panties coming out on the porch. Ellie was following right behind her, hanging on to Ida's undershirt with one hand and dragging a blanket behind her with the other.

For once they didn't say a word. I was thinking maybe they wouldn't notice it was Bobby's things in that fire.

They sat on the top step, one on each side of me. They was only half awake to start with, and the sight of them flames dancing was putting them back to sleep. I put an arm around each one and pulled Ellie's blanket up over our laps. And then I realized it wasn't Ellie's blanket—it was Bobby's.

I should have thought what to do next. But I didn't think at all. I just remembered that tiger jumping at me and screaming, "Polio germs!" All I could think was, *Bobby's blanket is full of germs.* I snatched the blanket away from the girls and jumped off the porch and threw it in the fire.

"Hey!" cried Ellie, suddenly wide awake. She jumped off the porch and run to the fire. "I want my blanket. Why are you burning my blanket?"

I jumped between her and the fire and held her back. "It's not your blanket," I yelled. "It's Bobby's and I can't let you have it. Where did you get it?"

"In the garden." Ellie was clawing at me. "I want Bobby's blanket!" She was trying to get to the fire and pushing me toward it. I felt the heat of it warming the back of my gown.

"It'll give you polio!" I yelled.

"I'll help you, Ellie," yelled Ida. She grabbed the broom off the porch and went toward the fire. She stuck the broom handle into the fire and reached for the blanket, but it was too late. Flames was licking it up. The broom handle hit the wooden barn. And when it did, Ida realized what I was doing.

"Stop it!" she screamed. "Stop burning my brother's play barn."

"And his teddy bear!" screamed Ellie.

Both girls started beating on me then. "You're burning Bobby's toys. What's he gonna play with? Ann Fay, you're so mean. I hate you, Ann Fay. I wish you was dead."

They screamed and pounded on me. I couldn't tell who was saying what, but I could tell they both hated me.

And I hated me too, so I let them push me to the ground and punch me. It felt good when they hit me. It felt like I deserved it. But I guess they wore out fast, because the next thing I knew they was laying on top of me, crying right along with me.

We laid there for the longest time, not saying a word.

After a while Ellie lifted her head and said real quiet, "Ann Fay, did you burn Pete too?"

"Oh, my Lord!" I sat up so fast I dumped both them girls onto the grass. "Where is that dog?"

In the middle of all the mess we was in, I had forgot all about Pete. The last time I seen him, he was laying on Bobby's blanket out in the garden, right before Bobby collapsed.

8

Outcasts!

July 1944

On Thursday I hopped out of bed almost before the sun did. I went through the kitchen to the back porch and dropped the bucket into the well. I took the wash basin off the nail on the wall, poured water into it, and splashed my face.

Then I woke the twins up and fixed them grits. "Hurry," I said. "Momma is expecting us to call at seven."

We took the shortcut through the fields along the edge of the woods that brought us to the Hinkles' back yard. We went to the back door like we always do. They have a sign there that says BACK DOOR FRIENDS ARE BEST.

Miss Pauline opened the door. She was fixing to say good morning. I could see the words forming on her lips, but they froze right there. Instead she covered her mouth and her nose with both hands and stepped back. "What are you doing here?" She sounded scared.

"Miss Pauline, I was wanting to use the telephone."

"But—but—you're under quarantine. You can't come in."

I never thought I'd hear Miss Pauline say I couldn't come into her house. She was the one that was always baking cookies and shoving them into our hands. And both her and Miss Dinah always said we was welcome to use their telephone anytime. Now here she was, acting like we had the bubonic plague or something. I was so surprised I couldn't think of a thing to say.

"I'm sorry," she said, her lips a-quivering. She pushed the door shut before I could even come up with another plan.

I do believe she was scared of us three harmless girls, and all because of Bobby having polio. I thought maybe if I tried to explain, or asked her to make the call ... I knocked on the door again. But she never did open it.

I put my arms around my sisters. "Let's go," I said. "I reckon we won't be talking to Momma after all." I heard my voice shaking. My eyes was stinging and if I wasn't careful the girls would catch me crying. I had to be the strong one.

But I didn't feel one bit strong.

We went home by the road. The blackberries was running rampant all over the side ditch. And the bright orange trumpet vine too. The road wasn't nothing but dry red dust under our feet. It splashed over my toes and covered the hairs on my toes so you could count every one of them if you was of a mind to.

But I wasn't in a mood for counting toe hairs. That was something I would do on a happy day. And even the blackberries and trumpet vine didn't make me happy today.

We passed the little church for coloreds that set by the side of the road. Two men was digging in their graveyard. I wondered if polio had killed one of their people. Or maybe it was a soldier that had died.

I thought how I lived less than a mile away from that colored church and I didn't know none of the people that went there.

Sometimes, on a Sunday evening, when I was sitting on the front porch watching Bakers Mountain turn deep blue as the sun went down the other side, I would hear them

BLUE

colored people singing, their voices floating over the fields. It was different from the singing at my church for sure. But I liked hearing it. And sometimes I'd go walking out the dirt road to catch the sound of it a little better. But I never went too close.

It seemed like there was just some neighbors you could get to know better than others—like Junior's family, for instance. When we got to their lane, I said, "Let's go talk to Junior. He'll know what to do."

Junior's hound dogs come out from under the porch and howled like they didn't have no idea who we was.

"Jesse, you hush and get over here right now," I hollered. Jesse started wagging his tail all sorry-like and slunk over to us. Ellie scooped him up and Ida sat in the dirt and started kissing on Butch, the other dog.

Junior must've been dozing on the porch swing because he looked downright sleepy. "Howdy," he said, and he give a big yawn.

"Junior," I said, "I got a predicament. I need to talk to Momma. But the Hinkle sisters won't let me use their telephone on account of the polio quarantine."

Junior stood up so fast the porch swing went flying out from behind him and then come frontward and almost knocked him over. "Well, that is plumb ridiculous!" he said. He opened the screen door and stuck his head inside. "Momma," he hollered, "I'm going to the Hinkles' to help Ann Fay make a telephone call." And without so much as another question about what was going on, he started down the steps.

One thing about Junior—whenever there's a problem, you can always count on him to take over.

I yelled at Ida and Ellie to quit playing with them dogs

and catch up to us. While we waited, Junior adjusted the straps on his overalls and tried to make his curly brown hair lay down by licking his hand and smoothing it across his head.

As we was walking I told Junior about Pete disappearing. "You seen him anywhere?"

Junior shook his head and frowned. "He might have run off somewhere to grieve," he said. "I've heard tell of dogs that was so sad when their owner disappeared all their hair fell out. Or they run off and died in private."

Ellie started crying when he said that. So Junior tried stuffing those words back in his mouth. "Course Pete wouldn't die," he said. "He's got too much spunk. He's probably out looking for Bobby right now. Shoot! That dog is so smart, he probably already found him."

Then he changed the subject real quick.

When we got back to the Hinkle sisters', Junior knocked on the front door and hollered out, "It's me, Junior Bledsoe. I need to talk to you, please, ma'ams."

Miss Pauline opened the door, but the instant she seen us standing behind Junior, she covered her face and stepped back.

"Please, Miss Pauline," Junior said. "Ann Fay needs to talk to her momma."

Miss Pauline said, "I'm sorry. But the health department put up those quarantine signs for good reason. She can't be breathing into our telephone. What if she has infantile paralysis and doesn't know it yet? The girls will have to get off our porch."

I tell you what's the truth—I felt downright dirty when Miss Pauline said that. I felt like one of them people in the Bible that had leprosy and wouldn't nobody but Jesus touch them. I took the girls by the hand, and we went out to stand by the yellow bell bushes at the edge of the yard.

Junior said, "What about I come in and talk to their momma? They can wait at the edge of the yard and I'll pass the messages back and forth."

Miss Pauline looked like she might actually let him do it. But then she said, "Maybe you've been touching the girls. You might have the germs too."

I seen Junior's shoulders sag and knew he was running out of ideas. But then he said, "Well then, can you call for us?"

Miss Pauline didn't say anything at first. I seen her eyes on us girls and I could see the fear in them. And the sadness too. She wasn't used to turning people away. Finally she said, "Tell me the number and I'll make the call for you."

Junior looked at the number on the letter and repeated it for Miss Pauline. Then he stood close to the dining room window and passed the messages back and forth.

Junior took over the conversation from the beginning. "Tell her Ann Fay is doing real good with them girls. She's just like a momma herself."

It wasn't true, of course. But it made me feel good that he was bragging on me so Momma wouldn't worry. And bad, because I didn't want to be a momma. Being the man of the house while Daddy was gone was one thing. But being the woman of the house—that was more responsibility than I could handle.

We couldn't hear Miss Pauline, but Junior said she told how Momma was going to stay at the hospital with Bobby as long as she could—that is, if Junior and his mother would help look after us. Of course Junior told Momma not to worry, on account of him and Bessie was already watching out for us.

BLUE

Ellie started crying for Momma then, and Ida went and put her arms around her. I patted Ellie on the head and smoothed down her blond hair, which was full of knots because we was in such a hurry to get to the telephone that we didn't comb it. She buried her face in my overalls and wiped her snot on them too. But I didn't fuss at her because I knew she was missing our momma.

And when it come to Bobby, she was probably as scared as me.

"Tell her the twins are doing fine," Junior told Miss Pauline. "Tell her they're standing right outside with Ann Fay and all three of them are smiling up a rainbow."

Junior Bledsoe could sure lie when he needed to. But I didn't fault him for it. I knew he didn't want my momma to worry.

I said, "Ask her does Bobby hate that iron lung?"

Junior passed the message on to Miss Pauline and waited for her to answer.

"He loves it!" said Junior, and I knew he was lying on my end too. "Your momma said it saved his life and he's too weak to be jumping around anyhow. He sleeps a lot."

Pretty soon Miss Pauline hung up the phone and shut the window. She motioned for Junior to come around to the back of the house. When he come back he had a stack of newspapers.

"Miss Pauline sent these," he said. "They tell all about that emergency hospital. She says if you come every day she'll give you the paper from the day before. Just get them off the back steps." Junior held up one paper so as I could see it.

The headline said YANKS PUSH FOE BACK IN FRANCE. I reached for the paper. I could use some good news about the war—something to make me feel like Daddy could come home alive.

And I did want to read all about the polio hospital.

"Well, it's not as good as talking to Momma," I said. "But at least it's something." Then I seen a smaller headline, lower on the page: *Boy, 12, Polio Patient, Dies at Camp Here.* My heart sunk to my dusty red toes.

I knew some people died from polio, but seeing it like that right here in my hometown paper and knowing Bobby was in the same hospital put a new fear right through me.

Junior carried most of them papers until Ellie started up whining about being tired. Then he said, "Here, Ann Fay, you take the newspapers and I'll carry her." He stooped down and said, "Get on my back, Ellie." And he carried her piggyback until Ida started asking when it was going to be her turn.

"When we get to that mailbox," said Junior.

I thought how Miss Pauline was so scared of us and here was Junior letting my little sisters breathe in his hair. Catching polio didn't seem to bother him a bit.

I hadn't never really thought of it before, but I figured out right then and there what is the definition of a true friend—someone who knows you might be dangerous to be around and they stick by you anyhow.

9

Hickory Daily Record
July–August 1944

With Momma gone to the hospital, all her jobs fell on me. I figured that included writing to Daddy about Bobby. I didn't want him worrying about us, but I knew he would want to know something as important as Bobby having polio.

So one day I finally sat down and wrote it straight out for him to see—although I tried to put a good face on it.

Dear Daddy,

We miss you something awful. I don't know if you heard about the polio epidemic. It got so bad they shut down a camp and turned it into an emergency hospital in Hickory.

Well, everybody says what happened next was a pure miracle. In just three days they had a regular hospital with beds and doctors and nurses. If that hospital needs any-thing, it just puts out a call. The donations start pouring in like water.

The bad news is, Bobby is there. He collapsed one day while we was working in the garden. He seemed fine one minute, but the next thing I knew, he couldn't move. Momma is there with him, so me and the girls are taking care of things around the house.

But don't worry about Bobby. They have polio doctors

from all over the country working there—even a doctor from the president's Warm Springs place. And smart people who study epidemics.

I read in the paper where <u>Life</u> *magazine even come and took pictures of the hospital, but I don't know when it will come out.*

Junior looks in on us every day, and of course I'm being the man of the house just like you told me. You would be proud of the garden, even if it does have more weeds than you can shake a stick at.

If Bobby was here he would say, "Good night, sleep tight, don't let the bedbugs bite." If I could, I would send you one of his pictures, but I had to burn them and his toys because of the polio germs.

Well, I better go now. But don't ever forget—I love you better than pinto beans and cornbread.

Your daughter,

Ann Fay

I sent that letter off with a prayer that the war would be over soon and my daddy would be home again. And Bobby and Momma too. All of us put back together.

But for now, I knew I had to make the best of it. In the evenings I read the newspaper—after I was done washing the clothes, cooking meals, and working in the garden.

I read everything in it, even the Colored News, which mostly told about their special church programs, like gospel quartets. And personal news, like who just sent their sons off to the war. It put me in mind of that colored soldier that got on the train the same time as my daddy.

Every day the paper had something on the front page about the polio hospital. One day it showed a picture of an iron lung. It looked like a big metal barrel on a stand. There was lots of buttons and meters on it and some little windows on the side—I reckon so the doctors and nurses could look in or maybe reach in and take care of the patient.

There wasn't nobody in it, so I couldn't really tell how my brother would look in one of them. And I for sure couldn't figure out how it worked. But I remembered how Junior said only a person's head would be sticking out. It made me feel all lightheaded just to think about my little brother being trapped in one of them. He should be running around in the back yard with Pete right now.

One thing I read in the paper just stuck with me. At the end of an article about that hospital it said, "The first case of polio was reported in Wilson County today. A thirteen-year-old white girl came down with the disease."

Well, I don't live in Wilson County, but the rest of it sounded like me. When I went to bed that night, I kept hearing that sentence in my head: *A thirteen-year-old white girl came down with the disease.* Those words floated in and out of my dreams and kept me half awake until I couldn't tell what was dreaming and what was real. I spent the night wiggling everything from my toes to my nose just to prove to myself that I didn't have polio.

When I woke up the next day I almost give up on reading that paper. But then Ida started pestering me to read it to her and Ellie. So sometimes I would tell them what it said. The good stuff, anyway.

"The polio hospital is bright and sunny," I told them. "It says they have really good doctors. And lots of volunteers—the women from the Hickory Country Club are providing food for the people at the hospital. It says they need baby beds and electric fans, but everything else has been donated."

"Like what?" asked Ellie.

"Like hotplates and sheets and lots of blankets for the Kenny treatments."

"What's the Kenny treatments?"

"I don't know," I said. "But I'm sure they make Bobby feel better."

It seemed like the epidemic was just getting worse. Every day the papers told about some camp or special program that was closed because of infantile paralysis. It even said the Catawba County schools wouldn't open on schedule. And that included Mountain View, our school.

At first the *Hickory Daily Record* had said the emergency hospital would be equipped for forty patients. But about three weeks later the paper said they had ninety patients. Volunteers was working around the clock, building new wards for all them people who had polio.

The polio news was always right there on the front page. And all around the polio news was articles about the war. I read the parts that wouldn't scare my sisters. Like when the Yanks—that's the American soldiers—took some city back from Hitler. If a soldier from Hickory got killed, I didn't dare mention it because the girls would think Daddy was dead. And to be honest, it always give me that feeling too. I knew it could be him any day.

We kept watching the mailbox for letters from Daddy. Even the girls could tell if he sent one or not, since it come in a special brown envelope. It was called V-mail—V for Victory. It had an oval-shaped window in it for our name and address to peek through. The letter was always in Daddy's handwriting, but it wasn't his ink—it was just a picture of the letter he wrote.

On the radio they said V-mail saved lots of money on

stamps. They said the army could take pictures of the mail and send it to the United States on a roll of film. Then they printed it out and sent it to the soldiers' families.

Daddy wrote back fast after I told him about Bobby.

My dear little children,

I know you have a heavy load to bear right now. But you know you can do whatever you put your mind to. Ida and Ellie, I'm counting on you helping Ann Fay. Don't make her do all the work.

Your momma is doing the right thing staying so close to Bobby, even though it's hard for you. If you need anything, be sure to call on Junior or Bessie. They'll do good by you.

Don't worry about me. The good Lord is keeping me safe, and I will come back to you just as soon as we get done fighting this war.

I reread your letters every chance I get. I pray for each one of you by name and I can see your sweet faces in my mind. Don't forget to pray for me.

Love,

Daddy

Daddy was right about Junior and Bessie Bledsoe. Junior come by every day to drop off some food Bessie had fixed or just to help me in the garden.

Sometimes the girls would help real good. But other times they come up with excuses like headaches and tummy pains. If they argued with me the least little bit, I'd back right down. I knew if I had let Bobby play when he wanted to, maybe he wouldn't be in that hospital right now.

The first corn and tomatoes got ripe while Momma and Bobby was at the hospital. I hated that because I knew

Momma had a hankering for tomato sandwiches and corn on the cob.

And speaking of tomato sandwiches—one day I broke a promise I made to Peggy Sue a long time ago. I took my little sisters for a picnic in Wisteria Mansion.

I don't know what got into me. I guess I got to thinking, what if Bobby never got to see that place? It would be a crying shame if a body had to go through this world without a glimpse of how beautiful it can really be. Not that I expected Bobby to die or anything. But the thought would cross my mind once in a while—especially at night when the house seemed so empty and quiet, when all I could hear was the twins stirring in their bed and the clock ticking on the wall and the crickets singing outside my window. Sometimes I would go curl up on the girls' bed just to feel them breathe.

I reckon I took the girls to the mansion on account of I was scared I might miss my chance if I didn't do it now. And then again, maybe I was just trying to escape to a place that was free of trouble.

Anyhow, we made tomato sandwiches. I even sprinkled a tiny bit of sugar over some blackberries and we packed them up and went off for some adventure.

"Where are we going?" asked Ellie.

"Back behind them vines to a special place where bad things don't happen."

Well, I reckon them girls needed to see a place like that as much as I did, because the next thing I knew, I was leading them with their eyes shut through the tangle of wisteria vines.

"Now," I said when we was inside the mansion with the thick wall of wisteria vines and the pine trees all around us. "Open your eyes."

"Ooooh," both girls said at the same time. From the way they stared, I could tell they never expected it to be so light and beautiful inside.

"Of course, it looks much better when the wisteria is blooming," I told them. "There's nothing in the world as beautiful as that. But you'll have to wait till next spring to see it."

The girls ran from room to room exploring all the nooks underneath the little groves of trees and pointing out the windows where there was gaps between branches.

After we ate our picnic, we crossed a log over the creek and followed a path that led to the river. By the time we got to the river they wanted worse than Christmas to get in the water. I did too, but I knew it was my responsibility to keep them out. "You heard what that doctor said on the radio. Stay out of the water, on account of most of the people who got polio was swimming or fishing before they got it."

"Huh," said Ida. "You just told us nothing bad ever happens in here."

"Yeah," said Ellie. "I'm fixing to get in the water."

Them girls had me there for a second. But I thought real fast.

"Well, that's true," I said. "But this river is the dividing line. And we ain't taking no chances. If you get close to that water I'll beat you with a hickory stick."

Sometimes I felt like I had turned into a mean old woman, what with my daddy going to war and my brother getting polio. Sometimes I wanted to rip them overalls right off and throw them in a fire. I didn't think no thirteen-year-old girl should have to burn her brother's toys and tell her sisters they couldn't go swimming in the river.

And that night at supper I was thinking I shouldn't be

eating sweet corn and tomatoes when my momma couldn't have any and might not even get a taste of them if she stayed at the hospital with Bobby all summer long.

But later, when I was drifting off to sleep, I remembered something I had heard on Junior's radio about farmers donating their garden foods to the polio hospital. And right then and there I started cooking up a plan.

10

Hospital Visit
August 1944

The next morning when I got the newspaper off the Hinkle sisters' back steps, I seen a brown paper sack there with my name on it. I opened it up and inside was six molasses cookies.

I looked up and seen Miss Pauline and Miss Dinah standing in the kitchen window. The two of them looked exactly alike with their dark glasses and their hair pulled back in a bun. Except Miss Dinah only come up to Miss Pauline's shoulder.

"Thank you!" I hollered. They was nodding and smiling and I could see they was trying hard to say sorry for the way things was with the quarantine. Which, if you want to know the truth, was off by then. That man from the health department had come and took the sign down about three or four weeks after he put it up. But that didn't mean them sisters was over their fear of polio.

I come home by way of Junior's house. I stood at the end of their lane and whistled the Bob White call.

Then I waited for him to whistle back—*Bob-bob-white.*

After I waited and whistled two more times, I heard him call me back. *Bob-bob-white.* He done it three times and each time it got closer. The next thing I knew, he was coming around the bend by the cedar trees.

"Hey," he said. "Is everything all right?"

"Yeah," I said. "But I need your help."

"You name it."

"Take me to the emergency hospital."

Junior shook his head. "Ann Fay, are you thick in the head? You know they ain't letting nobody in over there."

I grabbed his arm. "That ain't true. We heard on the radio where farmers are taking vegetables. I want to take some corn to my momma. And I could give a bushel of potatoes. I'm desperate for Momma and maybe I can even get a look at Bobby."

"They ain't gonna let you in. They got a policeman out there guarding the road. I heard that on the radio too."

"Junior, we gotta try. We'll tell them we just want to deliver the vegetables and leave again. You don't think we're gonna get polio from driving up to the building, do you?"

"How should I know? I hear tell people are covering their faces with their hankies and shutting their train windows when they go through Hickory."

"Well, that's just ignorant. And you are too, if you think I'm gonna let you talk me out of this. Don't you and your momma have some vegetables you want to give to the hospital?"

Junior's nose started twitching like it always does when he's nervous. Instead of answering me, he plucked one of them weeds that has a cone-shaped seed head. He made a loop out of the stem, pulled it tight, and shot the seed cone like an arrow over my head. He was stalling for time.

"Junior Bledsoe, are you going to help me or not?"

"I don't know, Ann Fay. I'm sure we could donate a peck of green beans. We just picked a bushel this morning. But even if Momma agrees, we ain't gonna get by with this."

"The least we can do is take a chance. If the hospital needs food, they ain't gonna be choosy about who brings it, are they?"

Junior didn't seem convinced, but he ain't good at saying no. So before the day was out, we was heading for town in my daddy's truck.

I wasn't planning to take Ida and Ellie with me. They was supposed to stay home and play in the yard, but Ida threatened to go wading in the creek while I was gone. So what choice did I have?

I don't know how Junior knew exactly where that hospital was, but one thing about Junior is, there ain't much he don't know. He drove straight to it. I was surprised to find it wasn't in town really—it was close to Lake Hickory, so close you could see the water. The closer we got, the more nervous I got.

Ida and Ellie bounced on the seat and chanted, "We're gonna see Bobby."

"Just put that idea right outta your head," I said. "Bobby is in an iron lung, and he sure ain't gonna be out in the yard where we can see him. Just be saying your prayers that we get a chance to see Momma."

Right when we turned on the road to the hospital, I seen a policeman standing there. He held up his hand for Junior to stop. Junior took a deep breath and said, "I hope you been saying your prayers, Ann Fay." He rolled down his window.

The police leaned in, looking us over like we was criminals trying to rob a bank, and asked, "Can I help you?"

I reckon I should've waited for Junior to speak, him being the man and all. But I leaned forward and said, "We brought some vegetables for the hospital. I heard you're accepting donations."

The police looked at Junior. "You can't just drive in here like this. Not with those girls in the car. It's not safe for them."

I thought he was talking about Ida and Ellie, so I said, "We can drop the young'uns off somewheres and come back."

You would've thought I wasn't even there, the way the police ignored me and spoke to Junior. "Take these three girls home and come back. I'm sure Mrs. Townsend will be grateful for the vegetables."

I was getting set to argue when Junior said, "Yes, sir." And just like that, he jammed the truck in reverse and backed out the road.

"Junior Bledsoe, what do you think you're doing?" I hollered. "You said you'd help me see Momma."

Junior didn't say a word and I thought for sure he was mad. When he got to the end of the road he backed out in the street and drove away.

Well, I was mad too. "You're crazy," I said, "if you think you're going back in there without me."

Junior set his jaw in a hard line and drove on down the road that went at an angle below the hospital. He pulled the truck over to the side of the road. "Well, that police ain't letting you in there, so I reckon you're gonna have to sneak in." He peered out the window past my head. I looked where he was looking. There was a slope covered with bushes and weeds by the side of the road. At the top of that slope, I could see the pine trees that surrounded the hospital.

And I could see what Junior was thinking.

All of a sudden I wanted to hug that boy's neck. "Yippee!" I said. "I'm climbing that hill." Then I remembered the twins. They had to get out of the truck too. I didn't see how all three of us could sneak in. But I opened the door and hopped out. I jerked my head so they would know to follow. "Come on."

"Are we gonna get caught?" asked Ida.

"No," I promised. "Not if you do what I say. Junior, you be sure to give me enough time to get up that hill before you go driving in there. I'll give the Bob White call when I'm getting close. You stay down here and listen till you hear it. Okay?"

Junior saluted me then and said, "Yes, sir!"

And I wasn't even wearing my overalls.

Wearing britches would've come in handy because there was a lot of blackberries on that hill. But I stomped down the briars and led the twins through.

We stomped and huffed and puffed our way up that hill, and every time one of the twins opened her mouth to speak I told her to hush or it would ruin everything. Finally we was at the top. I peeked through the tall grass at the edge and seen a rock building. It looked just like the newspaper described it. I was glad the police was out at the end of the road, but I knew someone else might catch me.

I turned and seen Junior parked right where we left him on the road. He had turned the truck around and was waiting for the signal.

Bob-white. I whistled so good I knew if that police or anyone else heard me, they would think it was a bird for sure. Junior started up the hill.

"Ida and Ellie," I said, "I might be able to sneak in close. But three of us would never make it. Some doctor or nurse would look out the window and see one of us for sure."

Well, it's a wonder some doctor didn't hear them right then and there, the way they both hollered. "Ann Fay, you promised we could see Momma!"

I clamped my hands over their mouths. "I did not. I only brought y'all along on account of you threatened to go wading in the creek. Now if you'll cooperate, I'll have a surprise for you."

Ida pulled her head away from my hand. "What kind of surprise? Ann Fay?"

I had to think fast. "Look," I said and I pointed out to the water. "Lake Hickory is right over there. If you wait behind these bushes till me and Junior come after you, we'll drive you over there. It's big as Bakers Mountain and I bet it's real cool under those trees."

The girls didn't make no promises to stay there. I glanced around and I couldn't see Daddy's truck no more. So I knew Junior had turned onto that road and was probably talking to that policeman right this minute. Somehow I had to make the twins stay in the weeds, and I didn't know how I was gonna do it. "Look," I said. "We still got sugar at home. If you stay right here and don't cause no trouble I'll make you a cake."

"Make a cake?" Ida whispered.

"Make a cake and take us to the lake?" asked Ellie.

I was getting real desperate because I knew Junior was probably fixing to unload those vegetables any minute. So I said, "Yes, make a cake and go to the lake."

"Hey," said Ellie. "That rhymes. 'Make a cake and go to the lake.'"

I pushed her down in the weeds and said, "Yes, it rhymes. Say it one hundred times real slow and maybe I'll be back by then. Now don't move, you hear?" Then I climbed over the top of the cliff and run to the nearest oak tree.

There wasn't many big oaks with trunks to hide behind. It was mostly young pines, so I was going to have a hard time

BLUE

staying out of sight. Suddenly I wished I had wore my brown dress instead of my light blue Sunday one.

About that time I heard a truck come around the back of the building. I peeked around the tree and seen it was Junior. He got out and knocked on the screen door at the back of the hospital. "Mrs. Townsend?" he called.

A woman come to the door, wiping her hands on her apron. "Yes?" she said through the screen door.

"I brung you some vegetables," said Junior. He pointed to the back of the truck, and when she looked to where he was pointing, I run two trees closer. I was real close now.

Mrs. Townsend pushed the door open and followed Junior down the steps and to the truck. "Did you grow these?" she asked.

"Yes, ma'am, I did," said Junior. I decided I was gonna choke him when I got the chance. I stepped out from behind that tree.

"Actually, I grew the potatoes and the sweet corn," I said. "It ain't enough for the patients, but maybe it will do for your kitchen help." I was still debating how I was gonna tell her my momma worked in her kitchen.

But then I didn't have to after all. I heard my momma's voice behind me. "Ann Fay?" I could hear how shocked and happy she was to see me. "How did you get here?"

The next thing I knew, my momma was clinging to me, tight as a chigger.

11

Pete
August 1944

At first I just hung on to my momma and leaned into her softness. She smelled like cooked greens and bacon. I buried my face against her and said, "I brought you some corn on the cob and tomatoes."

"Oh, honey," Momma breathed into my ear. "I can't believe they let you in."

"I just had to see you and Bobby."

Something changed in Momma when I said that about Bobby. She let out a little cry that put me in mind of Pete whenever one of us stepped on his foot by accident. And I felt her arms go real tight around me like one of them clamps Daddy uses to glue two pieces of wood together.

"Mrs. Honeycutt, is this your child?"

I turned around and seen it was that cook, Mrs. Townsend. Before Momma could answer, I heard a squealing, "Momma! Momma!" And the next thing I knew, Ida and Ellie was throwing themselves at her legs. They almost knocked her over and me too.

Momma was so startled she began to cry. I didn't know whether to fuss at Ida and Ellie for not listening or be glad for my momma that they was there.

But to tell the truth, I don't think Momma had more than two seconds to be glad any of us was there. All of a sudden people was coming from every which way, and my poor momma was standing there all red-faced with three young'uns hanging on to her.

"What's going on?" demanded a man in a uniform. He turned to Junior.

Junior threw up his hands. "I just brung some vegetables to the cook," he said. "I didn't bring these girls in. Honest to God!"

"We brought ourselves!" I said. "We wanted to see our momma and maybe wave to our brother. He's inside."

"No visitors allowed," said the guard. "You have to leave."

"Oh, please, sir," I heard my momma say. "Just let them stay a few minutes." She was hanging on to every one of us and dropping kisses on our heads like we was all she had in the world. Her fingers was digging into my arm.

That's when I got the same feeling I had at the train station that day. About our family and how it seemed like we was breaking apart. Her hugging me so desperate was giving me that bad feeling.

The guard took ahold of my arm. "It's not safe for any of you to be here," he said. "You have to leave."

I didn't argue with him. Suddenly I wanted to leave. I wanted to get away from Momma.

But Ida and Ellie latched on to Momma like a tick on our dog, Pete.

I grabbed both of them. "Stop making a scene. You don't wanna get Momma in trouble, do you?"

They wasn't paying no attention to me. "Help me, Junior," I called.

Junior come and unwrapped Ida's arms from Momma's legs, and by the time I had Ellie loose, he had the truck door open and was shoving Ida inside. I carried Ellie kicking and screaming and pushed her in too. Then I climbed in and pulled the door shut quick before they could climb back out. We was all in a sweating, squirming heap when Junior climbed in the other side, cranked up the truck, and shoved it into gear.

I got a last look at Momma just before we went around the corner of the building. She was standing there with her mouth open, wiping loose hairs away from her face and looking like she had got a visitation from an angel.

Junior was driving fast—too fast for the hospital grounds—and there was plenty of people running out to see what was going on. All of a sudden he hit the brakes hard and I seen that a little black dog had run across the road right in front of him.

It took me a second to realize it was our dog. I couldn't believe my eyes. I never thought I'd see that dog again. "Pete! It's Pete!" I hollered. "Stop and get him, Junior. Let's take him home."

But Junior wasn't stopping for nobody—not even the policeman that stopped him on the way in. The policeman's eyes nearly popped out of his head when he seen us girls in that truck with Junior. It was a crazy, scrambled ride. The girls was crying and we was all smushed up against each other, me sitting half on top of both of them.

I hung on to the dashboard till we were out of the road that led to the hospital. "Junior," I said, "you were right about Pete. He followed Bobby to the hospital. Did you hear me, girls? Pete ain't dead. He's back there watching over Bobby."

It felt good to hear myself say it. I just knew Bobby would get better with Pete there being his guardian angel.

All of a sudden I felt good—like I had climbed a mountain. I had actually got to see Momma and take her some corn and tomatoes. I knew I should fuss at Ida and Ellie for not staying put in them weeds like I told them to, but instead I felt like celebrating. So I said, "Junior, take us to the lake."

"I'm taking you straight home and don't say a word about it," said Junior. He kept glancing in his mirror like he thought the town of Hickory was fixing to send the police after him.

When we got home, I used the last of our sugar to make a cake for the twins. Then I took some old copies of the *Hickory Daily Record* and the cake out to the corncrib. We set up some sweet-potato crates for tables and chairs and had us a regular playhouse. Ida and Ellie ate the cake while I read the paper to them.

"Look!" I said. "It says right here that the president's wife was on the train in Hickory. It says about a hundred people was watching for her to come stand on the platform and wave at them."

"Did she do it?"

"No, she didn't. But they seen her in the dining car."

Wow! It didn't seem possible that President Roosevelt's wife had rode right through little old Hickory. I wondered if the president would ever go through. I'd give my overalls just to get a glimpse of Franklin D. Roosevelt.

While I was reading the paper, I seen a reminder that there was a paper shortage because of the war. We was supposed to turn in every last bit of paper we could find so it could be reused. So after we ate the cake and played for a while, I went inside and gathered up all the newspapers and put them in order by the date.

All of a sudden, something caught my eye that I had missed before. There on the first page on July 4—right where I don't know how I could've missed it—was a story about our dog. Of course, the story didn't mention Pete by name, but it had to be him, on account of it was in the paper right after Bobby went to the hospital—when Pete disappeared. And now we had seen him there with our own eyes.

"Ida!" I called. "Ellie! Come here and look at this."

The girls come running into the living room and I read it to them.

DOG FOLLOWS POLIO VICTIM TO HOSPITAL

To a little black terrier who has stationed himself out at the Emergency hospital the word polio is some mysterious something which keeps his young master away from home.

According to the nurses at Health Center the mangy looking pup arrived Saturday and evidently has every intention of staying until his master is released.

The dog has burrowed a pint-size fox hole in which he sleeps at night, and wags his tail thankfully when the nurses throw him bits of food during the day.

The hospital has a strict no-visiting rule, but the self-appointed canine sentry has taken matters in his own paws.

Besides being a man's best friend, he figures that rules for human conduct don't apply to a fellow's dog.

"That's our dog!" squealed Ida.

"Pete's in the newspaper," said Ellie. "Ann Fay, why didn't you tell us?"

"I didn't know he was in the paper. I just now seen this."

"But you read the paper every day," said Ida.

"And you skip things so we won't cry," said Ellie.

"I didn't know nothing about Pete being at that hospital. I was so upset about Bobby I didn't even miss that dog till you mentioned him. I betcha he hopped in the back of that hearse and hid there till it got to the hospital. That dog is too smart for his mangy britches."

"How come Momma didn't tell us about Pete?"

"Well, if you ain't noticed," I said, "we can't exactly talk to her. Besides, I think she's keeping it a secret. If that hospital finds out whose dog it is, they might take a notion to send him home again. Momma probably wants him there close to Bobby."

"Is Bobby gonna come home soon?"

That bad feeling hit me again when Ida asked it. But I said what she wanted to hear. "Yeah," I said. "He'll be home real soon. And Pete and Momma will too."

"And Daddy? Is Daddy coming home?"

"Of course," I said. "Ain't that what he says in his letters? He's going to win that war, and before you know it he'll be back. Then we'll all be together again."

It was easy to say what my sisters wanted to hear. But I didn't feel so sure of any of it.

That night when I put the girls to bed, we prayed for God to bring Bobby and Daddy home safe, just like we prayed every night. Then I went outside and sat on the front porch and looked up at the moon. I imagined God was sitting on the top edge of it with His legs hanging over the sides.

So I didn't bother to close my eyes. I just looked at the moon and talked to Him. "What's happening to us?" I asked. "When we sent Daddy off to the war, I felt like our family was breaking apart. And today I felt it again. Why did I feel like that today when Momma was squeezing me so hard?

Oh, God, please, please, keep us together."

I thought praying was supposed to make me feel better, but all I could feel was Momma's fingers digging into my arms and her hanging on to us three girls like we was all she had left in the world.

12

The Hearse Comes Back

August 1944

Not even a week after we seen Momma at the hospital, that big black hearse drove up to our house again.

Ida and Ellie was playing hopscotch in the dirt and I was picking green beans in the garden. Momma was in the front seat, but I didn't see no sign of Bobby. I went running to the car to see if they had him laying in the back.

But then I seen Momma's face and she wasn't smiling. When I got to her door, she just sat there, unraveling the blue trim she had crocheted onto her handkerchief. She didn't look at me. But I could see her eyes was all red from crying.

Ellie and Ida was crowded up to the car door, asking for Bobby. I pulled them back and said, "Let Momma out. Can't you see Bobby ain't with her?"

I could see they was fixing to hit her with a flood of questions. But even with the door shut and the window rolled up, she was shrinking away from them like she was scared of her own young'uns. So I just blurted it out, which I should not have done. But it's not like I had time to plan the right way to say such a terrible thing. So I just said it fast and straight.

"Bobby ain't coming home. He's dead."

And even if I did know it in my heart already, it still got me by surprise. I still felt like somebody had put a knife in my stomach.

I held the girls back while the driver helped Momma into the house. She sunk into the sofa and didn't say a word. Ida and Ellie was hanging on to her, begging her to say it wasn't true. She didn't answer them one way or another. Instead, she shrunk herself into the corner of the sofa till it seemed like she was smaller than the twins.

The man stood at the screen door. "Where should I put your boy?" he asked.

That's when I knew they had brought his body home and we was going to bury him ourselves.

Momma just stared at her raggedy handkerchief and didn't bother to answer. So he turned to me.

"Does he have a box?" I asked.

The man shook his head and looked kind of sorry. "No, I offered. But your momma said you couldn't afford it."

I didn't know what to say about where to put my dead brother. I couldn't stand the thought of carrying him into the house. Bobby always slept with me, and I was afraid that if I laid him on my bed I wouldn't ever be able to sleep there again.

I run and got a baby-sized crazy quilt that Grandma Honeycutt had made. I folded it and laid it on the porch floor. Then the man opened the back of that hearse and laid my brother out on that quilt with all them colors and shapes and zigzaggy stitches. And I kept thinking how him dying didn't make no more sense than the design in that quilt.

At first I couldn't even look at him. I didn't want to see what my baby brother looked like dead.

But that man put his hand on my shoulder. "Is there anything I can do?" he asked. And I knew he wanted to leave and go on with his life—whatever that was.

So I forced myself to look at Bobby.

In some ways it wasn't so bad. His face was round and cute as ever. His curly brown hair had got almost as long as a girl's while he was at the hospital. But his legs and arms and body was skinny and shriveled up to nearly nothing.

After the man laid him on the quilt, I didn't have no idea what to do next. All I could think of was to run for Junior. But I just couldn't leave the twins alone like that, with Bobby's dead body on the porch and Momma coming apart like that handkerchief she was picking at.

So I asked the man, "Will you take my sisters to Junior's house on the way out? It's just up the road a piece. They know where he lives, and he'll know what to do."

Ida threw both arms around my waist and screamed, "No! I ain't getting in that car." Ellie grabbed onto both of us and said she wasn't neither. So I hobbled as best I could to the car with them stuck onto me like that. I started pulling their hands loose.

"Help me," I said. "They're whiners, but once they get to Junior's you won't have to worry with them no more."

Somehow we shoved the twins in. As they was driving away, I seen them clinging to the dashboard and looking all scared toward the back of that car. That's when I realized I had just shoved my sisters into a hearse.

I reckon they must have been terrified of what else was in there. Well, I knew the closer they got to Junior's house the safer they would feel, so I didn't try to stop that car.

Suddenly the world was so quiet I could hear the grasshoppers clicking around in the yard. A crow cawed just like it was any other day when I was in the garden or hanging out the wash.

I sat down on the porch floor beside my dead brother and listened to the birds and insects. A fly walked across

BLUE

Bobby's eyelids. I shooed it away. It come back, but I stayed right there and waved my hand over his face every time it tried to land.

I looked at Bobby's thin little body that had lost all its chubbiness while he was shut up in that iron lung. I seen close up what polio can do to a person.

How was I going to explain this to my daddy? Somehow I knew if he was here, he would've stopped it. But he put me in charge and I messed everything up.

I thought how Daddy told Bobby to play some every day and Bobby was doing his best to listen to him. But I made him work till he dropped.

My tears started dripping onto Bobby's face and running down his cheeks and into his ears. I didn't wipe them off because I knew he was cold and I couldn't bear to feel the coldness. I just wanted to remember him warm and snuggly.

I could still feel how he would climb onto my lap and beg me for a story. And I could hear how he giggled when I told him his pictures was so good they should be put in a magazine.

Then I remembered that I had burned every last one of his pictures. Now what was I going to remember him by? The crying overtook me then, and next thing I knew, I was laying half across him, sobbing like a baby.

And his body cooled me like the creek does on a hot summer day. I didn't even hear Junior drive up in Daddy's truck, but all of a sudden I felt Bessie's big arms around me. She hugged me like a momma and I felt her rocking me like a big cushiony rocking chair.

She kept saying, "Have mercy. Have mercy on this poor child." At first I thought she was talking about Bobby. But then I knew she was talking about me because she said, "She's just a young girl and life has hit her so hard already. Have mercy."

13

The Funeral

August 1944

While Bessie was rocking me, I heard the screen door open and Momma come out on the porch. She reached for Bobby, so I got up and let her have him. She went and sat on the steps with him hugged up against her like he was sleeping on her lap. Only he didn't curl up against her the way he always done. He just hung there like one of the twins' paper dolls that don't care nothing about the person that's playing with it.

Ida and Ellie crowded in on either side of Momma. When Ellie felt how cold Bobby was, she come back and got the quilt and covered him up. Momma wrapped it around his body and cuddled him like he was a newborn and said, "Hush, honey, don't cry."

But I didn't know who she was talking to, because every one of us was crying.

Then Bessie went and knelt on the porch floor behind my momma and put her arms around her and said, "Have mercy." She leaned her forehead into the back of Momma's hair and said, "We stopped by the Hinkles' to use the telephone. Reverend Price will be here soon."

Momma nodded, and I thought she looked grateful.

Bessie said, "I'm going inside and cook y'all a good meal. Junior is out back looking for some wood to build a box for Bobby."

I knew Daddy had some cedar boards in the shed because he had made a wardrobe for Momma last Christmas. So I started around the side of the house to see if I could help. It was better than watching my momma suffer.

Junior was dusting off them leftover boards when I got there. He had put on his best blue jeans and a blue plaid shirt like he was going to town. I picked up a rag and started helping him. He didn't look at me or say a word.

When his daddy died, I didn't know what to say neither. Now I thought how Bessie was the one who always knew the right thing to say. *Have mercy.* It didn't try to make you feel better or explain something that couldn't be explained. It just felt like a prayer.

I spoke up to save Junior the trouble. "Daddy was gonna build Pete a doghouse from these boards," I said. "When he comes home from the war."

"I don't reckon Pete come home with your momma, did he?" asked Junior.

"No," I said. "Leastways, I didn't see him."

I could tell from the way Junior was eyeballing them boards that he was trying to figure how long to cut them. I knew he didn't want to go around to the front porch and measure Bobby for his coffin. "Wouldn't surprise me a bit," he said, "if that dog would come dragging in here to sleep on Bobby's grave. Dogs have a way of knowing these things."

I picked up a board and set it on end to make sure it come up to my waist. I knew exactly how high Bobby was, standing next to me. "This one's a good length," I said to Junior. "Use it."

So that's what we used to cut the others by. Junior put the boards across the porch with the extra part hanging out over the edge. I sat on them to hold them still while he cut them with Daddy's handsaw.

The sawdust settled like snow on Junior's black shoes.

When it come time to hammer them boards together, I made Junior let me take a turn. I needed to hit something, and them nails was convenient. I imagined polio germs was on them nailheads. I hit them hard and straight.

It done something for me to smack them nails. It was like being mad took the place of hurting—for a while, anyway.

When the box was all nailed together, I went and got a can of oil from the cellar steps. I rubbed oil into the wood just like Daddy did on Momma's wardrobe, and it give the box a nice shine. Then Junior and I carried it around to the front porch. Momma was still there trying to cuddle with Bobby and using her thumb to push his curls behind his ears.

Reverend Price was there too. He had brought his wife, Mavis, with him, and Lottie Scronce too. Lottie is the woman from church whose two boys was killed in the war. Now here she was, standing with them other church people around the bottom of the steps, patting my sisters on the head and not saying much. Tears was dripping off her trembly chin. Then all of a sudden, just like she done at church every Sunday, she snapped open her pocketbook and pulled out a mint candy for each of my sisters.

The preacher was trying to make arrangements for the burial, but Momma wasn't saying much. Sometimes she would nod, like when Reverend Price suggested digging the grave under the mimosa tree. "I think it'll be easier to dig there," he said.

But I knew he was looking at the lacy leaves and feathery pink blossoms and thinking how it would always be a pretty site.

Junior set the cedar box on the porch floor, and I took the quilt and folded it so it would fit inside. I made a little pillow for Bobby's head. And Lottie Scronce put a mint candy inside. She'd given Bobby one every Sunday since he was two years old, so I reckon she wanted to do it one last time.

Reverend Price asked me for a shovel, so I took him around back and let the women help Momma put Bobby in that cedar box.

I got the shovel from where it hung over two nails on the shed wall. Junior found a pickax, and the three of us walked down to the mimosa tree. We took turns digging, and I dug just as good as the men did because I was madder than both of them put together.

And besides, I had to do Daddy's part.

By the time Reverend Price decided it was deep enough, his white shirt was soaked plumb through and had smears of red dirt on it. He pulled a comb and a handkerchief out of his back pocket and made himself look like a preacher again while Junior and I drunk water from the dipper in the bucket on the back porch. Bessie brought the preacher a cup of cold water from the refrigerator.

I went inside and pulled on my blue Sunday dress. Then I grabbed Ida's and Ellie's navy blue dresses with the white pinafores and shoved them over their heads while they sobbed.

"Slick your hair down," I said. I run a brush through mine and got a barrette out of the little cedar box my daddy made for me last Christmas. I seen a dime and two pennies laying there in the box. They put me in mind of the pennies Daddy give Bobby when he went away. I thought how Bobby hung on to them like they was his last piece of bread.

I took those pennies out of my box and went to the porch and put one in each of Bobby's hands. "There you go, Bobby," I said. "That's from your daddy."

But they slid right out of his hands onto that crazy quilt.

When everybody was all set, Reverend Price and Junior carried Bobby's box on their shoulders down to the grave. Ida and Ellie walked between them with their hands stretched up, barely touching the box with their fingertips but still trying their best to carry Bobby one last time. The rest of us followed so quiet all you could hear was our feet crunching on the dry grass. We stood around the grave, and Junior and the reverend wiggled the box into the hole.

I reckon the funeral home would've done a better job, but I know it would not have been done with as much love as we put into it. Every one of us took turns shoveling dirt on that box.

Mavis Price started singing "Amazing Grace" and Bessie joined in, singing the harmony. They stood there like two opposites—Mavis thin and neat with her white lace collar and her blue hat, and Bessie large and soft with her green flowered dress and Momma's pink apron. It was smeared with flour and food stains, and Bessie's dark hair had some flour in it too.

It really surprised me when I heard my momma singing, and the next thing I knew, I was singing along. I reckon we all sung a part of it at one time or another. Mavis sung every word of every verse in a voice pure as an angel's.

Then Reverend Price quoted the shepherd's psalm and we all joined in on account of we had memorized it in Sunday school. Reverend Price said some words that no one had memorized—things only a preacher would know—about

BLUE

the ways of God and how we don't understand them. About the waters passing over us and how God promises he'll be with us anyway.

He asked us did anybody want to say some words about Bobby, and I just kept thinking, *Good night, sleep tight, don't let the bedbugs bite.* But it didn't seem like the right thing to say, so I didn't.

But then Momma surprised me by saying it herself. She told how Bobby said that every night to the nurses at the polio hospital.

She said the nurses loved Bobby like he was their own, and when the electricity went out in the middle of a lightning storm, one of them cranked his iron lung by hand for over an hour till the lights come back on. "She saved Bobby's life," said Momma.

For a while, anyway.

That started up a bunch of questions about the polio hospital. Mavis Price asked how come the emergency hospital let her bring Bobby home. "Weren't they worried about you bringing polio germs home?" she asked.

"I don't think so," said Momma. "People come and go from the hospital every day, you know. And I never got into the contagious ward—not even when Bobby was in there. But still, I had to get permission from the health officer before I could bring him."

Ida wanted to know why didn't Pete come home from the hospital with Bobby. Momma threw her hand over her mouth and said, "Oh, my Lord, I forgot about Pete. You know, the whole time I was there, I never told them he was our dog. But I called him by his name, and next thing I knew, everyone was calling him Polio Pete."

Momma said the nurses would sneak good chicken meat

to Pete. "It got to where Pete was everybody's dog," she said.

I think we was all just so glad that Momma was talking again. Mavis Price took her by the arm and the next thing I knew we was all wandering up to the house and singing, *"I'll fly away, oh glory."*

Bessie laid out such a spread on the table that a body wouldn't hardly believe there was a war on. We had mashed potatoes, cured ham, green beans, tomatoes, and biscuits with blackberry jelly.

The blackberries put Momma in mind of another story about the emergency hospital. She said back in June when it was still a health camp for children who'd been sick, Mrs. Earle Townsend promised the campers that if they picked blackberries, she'd make cobbler. Well, she was mixing up the batter when the telephone rang. It was Dr. Whims, the county health officer. He told Mrs. Townsend the campers had to leave in thirty minutes so it could become a polio hospital.

"Well," said Momma, "Mrs. Townsend said she couldn't possibly send the children home without their blackberry cobbler. So Dr. Whims gave her forty-five minutes instead. When those children got back with the berries, they started packing their clothes while Mrs. Townsend did the baking. They were eating cobbler when the cars started lining up outside to take them home.

"Mrs. Townsend never did leave," Momma continued. "She stayed right there and became the hospital cook."

I looked at us crowded around our little kitchen table with two people on either side and someone at every corner with their knees straddling the table legs. I got to thinking how amazing it was that these people was there, laughing and talking with us after so many weeks with just us three girls.

It was kind of strange that we was laughing on the day of my brother's funeral. But then again, most of these people had lost their own family members, and maybe that was why they was so good at bringing comfort to other people.

But all of a sudden, right in the middle of a hearty laugh over something Junior had said, Momma got real quiet and laid down her fork. She got up from the table and went outside on the back porch. We watched her go, and our laughing turned to pure quiet and followed her out the door.

14

The Plan

August 1944

That's how it was with Momma after Bobby died. Some days she'd fix breakfast and clean the house and make sure the twins washed their faces and brushed their teeth. On them days, my sisters would tag after her like twin puppy dogs. They'd beg for stories about Bobby, but whenever she told one, they'd start crying.

So she'd sit down and pull them onto her lap and sing, *"Hush, little baby, don't say a word, Papa's going to buy you a mockingbird."* It was a silly song that didn't make no sense, but it hushed them girls up every time. And it even brought comfort to me. Pretty soon I was thinking Momma had turned into her old strong self again.

But then I'd look up from picking cucumbers and see her sitting by Bobby's grave, shaking the twins off like they was a couple of pesky flies buzzing around her face.

I'd holler at the girls to come help me in the garden, and sometimes they did because Momma was ignoring them anyhow. But Ida got to where she started getting tummy aches every time it suited her. I knew she was just trying to get out of work. But it done the trick for sure. I wasn't taking no chance on one of them coming down with polio on account of me and that garden.

It seemed like there was one thing and then another

with that garden. About the time the vegetables was almost done, the wisteria out behind them sneaked across Daddy's ditch and started reaching for the dry cornstalks. Even if the garden was practically finished, I couldn't let the wisteria take it over.

I wasn't ready to declare war on it, but I knew I had to cut it back past the ditch. What would I tell Daddy if he come home and found that wisteria growing in his garden?

I wasted a big part of my day putting off the job of cutting it back. I knew by now, I couldn't do more than slow it down. Cutting it back wouldn't bring down the mansion in the woods. It wouldn't change anything, really. Still, I didn't want to do it.

But Daddy had left me in charge of his jobs. I had done some hard ones already—watching the girls for weeks while Momma was gone, burning Bobby's toys and digging his grave. I told myself that cutting wisteria was nothing compared to those things.

I just didn't feel like doing one more hard thing.

Finally I did what I had to do. I got Daddy's scythe out of the shed and started working. I tried to swing it through a whole bunch of vines, but they got tangled on my blade. I hacked and the blade just bounced off the tough vines.

And the worst part was the way the vines wrapped themselves around the branches of the cherry tree by the garden's edge. I had to get them out of the tree. I twisted and pulled and yanked and cut and made only the least bit of progress.

The sweat dripped off my eyelids and the tip of my nose. I stopped to wipe my face on my sleeve, and I studied the wisteria while I rested.

For the first time I saw wisteria the way my daddy seen

it. It might be beautiful for a few weeks each spring, but here in the middle of the summer, with it taking over whole trees and marching into the garden, it seemed like a pure curse.

Wisteria used to make me feel nothing but happy. But suddenly I saw why it put my daddy in such a blue mood.

I hadn't wanted to see it his way. I wanted to think of it only as the beautiful wall to my mansion. I wanted to hang on to sunny days with sweet purple petals raining down on me and Peggy Sue.

But now I had to think like the man of the house. I had responsibilities that I never asked for. It seemed like fun days were gone forever.

I felt a huge sadness just thinking about all the good things I lost since my daddy went off to war. Daddy himself, to start with. And fun family times like swimming in the river and hiking up Bakers Mountain. Bobby. Picture shows with Peggy Sue. Going anywhere just for fun.

My whole childhood—if you want to know the truth.

I had no intention of crying, so I fussed at the wisteria instead. I yelled while I whacked. "You think you can take over the whole dad-gum world, don't you? Just like Hitler, swallowing up one country after another. Just like polio. Grabbing one baby and then going for the next one. You know what? I hate you!"

I let all the pain about Daddy and Bobby come out against my beloved wisteria. I whacked. I sliced at it. I tried to break the vines with my bare hands, but I only rubbed my garden blisters open. My hands hurt so bad I finally stopped and just looked at them vines.

I had this feeling that if I stared at it long enough, I could see the wisteria growing. Or hear it, maybe. I had to come up with a better plan. I decided to stop for the time being.

I reckon I scared Ida and Ellie with all that screaming, because they actually helped me pick the last of the green beans. I took the beans to Momma and dumped them right there by Bobby's grave. "Here," I said. "How about you string these beans while I pick the okra? I'll get you a knife."

I got me a knife too, to cut the okra. I put on Daddy's long-sleeved garden shirt and buttoned the cuffs so the okra wouldn't make me itch. Then I went to the shed to get his work gloves.

It was cooler in the shed, and the smell of it was the smell of Daddy after he run the tiller or crawled out from under the truck when he changed the oil. I stood there and sucked in the smell of dirt and oil till it pulled me to the dirt floor.

"Oh, Daddy," I moaned. "I know you're counting on me. I'm doing my best, but it's so hard."

Next thing I knew, I was crying. I cried till my head hurt and my throat ached and I didn't have a speck of energy left in me. I wanted to stay in the cool, dark shed that smelled like Daddy. If I stayed long enough, maybe Momma would come looking for me.

But Momma wasn't worrying about me. She had got used to me taking care of her. It was like I was her momma, instead of the other way around.

I knew I had to go, and I knew what Daddy would say if he was there. "It's the first step that's the hardest," he always said. So finally I wiped my eyes and my nose on Daddy's shirttails. I pushed my hair out of my face and picked up the knives and drug myself out to the mimosa tree. Momma was still sitting there, with her hair all scraggly around her face and her legs stretched out in front of her and her dress shoved up to her knees.

After all those times she told me to sit like a lady, I

had a notion to say the same to her. But she was so out of heart, just dragging one of the last wilted mimosa blossoms through the red dust with no gumption at all. I just couldn't be mean to her.

I held out the knife, and she looked at it like it was some object I brought from halfway around the world.

"Take it," I said. "We got beans to can. And I still have to pick the okra, so you've got to string the beans."

I seen I would have to get her started. I took off Daddy's shirt, used it to wipe the sweat off my neck, and then sat on it.

"Look, Momma," I said. "This here's how you do it. Remember? You're the one that showed me in the first place."

I wanted to get the canning done so I could read the paper. I wanted to check the war news to see if Daddy was making progress over there. And read the next chapter of the continued story.

"Momma," I said, "you know how you used to read the story in the newspaper, a new chapter each day? Well, I'm reading it now. This month it's called *Hometown Girl*." And then I started telling her the story. I handed her beans while I talked. "Good girl," I said whenever she strung one.

I bet I strung ten beans to every one of hers. But at least she done something. And while we was stringing, I told her the whole story of *Hometown Girl* from the very first chapter.

"So if you want to know the rest," I said, "I'll read it to you. But not till every bean is in a jar lined up on the windowsill."

When the beans was strung, I picked the okra. If I put it off till tomorrow, those pods would be twice as long and three times as tough.

The next morning Momma washed the clothes and scrubbed the floors, and I thought maybe she was going to be all right after all.

But the next thing I knew, she was carrying the family picture around, hugged up to her chest. The picture was taken in front of Daddy's truck. Bobby had his hands over his face because the sun was in his eyes. Every time I looked at it I wanted to reach in and move his hands. And now, that picture, where you couldn't even see him good, was all Momma had to remember him by.

It was all my fault—for working him to death and then burning his things.

My sisters, who was clingy from the day they was born, got to where they wouldn't let go of Momma's skirt tails, even when she curled up on her bed or threw herself on Bobby's grave. It was bad enough seeing Momma on that grave so much of the time. But seeing my sisters there too— well, that just made me want to take off through the wisteria and never come back.

But I knew by now, there was no such thing as a place where bad things couldn't touch you.

One day about a week after we buried Bobby, I got to thinking how even with the war on, Daddy managed to take us every summer to Mamaw and Papaw Honeycutt's in Georgia. So I got this idea. I took the bicycle out of the shed and rode over to Junior's to get some help. Him and his momma was shucking corn under the sweet gum tree when I got there. I dropped my bicycle beside the tree and picked up an ear of corn and started shucking too.

"Have mercy, child, I hope you didn't come over here to work," said Bessie.

"Well," I said, "I might as well help you out, since I come to ask for a favor."

"Well, you know me and Junior will do whatever we can. How's your momma today?"

"She's just like having another child around," I said. "And Ida and Ellie are like two babies, crying all the time. You can't blame them either with all they been through. But I'm still thinking it's time to do something. I got a plan."

Junior flicked a worm off the corn he was shucking and said, "Lord help us all, Ann Fay. When you get a plan, why do I want to run the other way?"

"Oh, Junior, I know you wouldn't mind getting outside of Catawba County and seeing a thing or two."

"Just like I thought. This has something to do with your daddy's truck."

"Look," I said, "if you don't want to help out, I'll just drive it myself. I'm thinking it would do us all good if Ida and Ellie was to go to Georgia and spend some time with Mamaw and Papaw Honeycutt. Mamaw will make over them like they're the greatest thing since the radio. And that's exactly what they need."

"Honey," said Bessie, "if your sisters need a little loving, just bring them here and let me look after them for a while. I can love on them just as good as their own grandmother."

I put my shucked ear of corn in Bessie's big metal dishpan and picked up another one. "I thought about that," I said. "But it's just too close. They need to go someplace where they can't come whining home every day."

Junior shook his head. "Georgia and South Carolina aren't letting people from the polio area into their states."

"I know that," I said. "I read it in the paper. But like Daddy always says, 'Where there's a will, there's a way.' And by gum, I got the will."

"Well," said Junior, "I'm just dying to hear about your *way*, Ann Fay."

"The way is, you're gonna sneak us in," I said. "We won't

see anybody, so we won't pass out any germs. Not that we got any germs in the first place. We'll go at night when our license plate won't be so noticeable. All we gotta do is take some back roads across the state line. And me and Ida and Ellie will be in the back of the truck under a canvas. We'll put something back there to hide behind, some furniture or hay or something. If anybody asks what you're doing, you tell them you're taking a load to the kinfolks in Georgia."

"Oh, great, I get to do the explaining!" said Junior. "And what about gas? We don't have enough ration stamps to get us all the way to Georgia."

"Well then," I said, "Mamaw and Papaw can meet us halfway. In South Carolina."

"Why not all the way? Why don't they just come up here and stay with your momma and help take care of them girls?"

"Because there's a war on, that's why. My papaw runs the feed mill down there, and he's short on help as it is. He's even had Mamaw helping out part-time. I just know they couldn't come."

Bessie said, "I'll stay with your momma while you and Junior take those young'uns to South Carolina."

"But Momma," said Junior.

"Don't 'But momma' me, young man. Can't you see Ann Fay needs our help? And we're going to give it to her." Bessie picked up a butcher knife and whacked off the thick green stem of a corncob.

Junior jumped back, but the white juice of that corn still splattered all over his face.

15

The Escape
August 1944

I talked Junior into going to Peggy Sue's to call Mamaw Honeycutt for me. "You can't use Pauline Hinkle's telephone for this," I said. "She'd lay awake nights thinking she should turn us in to the police."

"And what makes you think Peggy Sue's mother is gonna let us get by with it?"

"She don't have to know. Just tell Peggy Sue and she'll call as soon as she gets a minute to herself. She'll love pulling off a secret like that."

Junior finally agreed. To save gas for the trip, he walked the four miles to Peggy Sue's house.

"Tell her we're not under quarantine now," I said. "Just in case her momma decides to take us to the movies again." I didn't expect Mrs. Rhinehart to get brave about polio now, but I figured it wouldn't hurt to try.

I had got a letter from Peggy Sue right after Bobby died. She said her momma wouldn't have let her come to Bobby's burial even if she had found out in time. Some people was more scared of the epidemic than others was. Mrs. Rhinehart was one of the scared ones.

I went home to tell the twins they was going to Georgia. I listed off the good things about visiting Mamaw Honeycutt. "You can play dress-up in her attic," I said. "And she'll make you banana pudding and read Bible stories to you at night. And Papaw will take you along to the feed mill and give you one of them lollipops he hands out."

I reckon them things sounded like more fun than trailing after Momma. All of a sudden Ida jumped up and started pulling her Sunday dress and panties out of the bureau drawer.

For once, I was glad Momma was in one of her faraway moods. When I told her I was taking the girls to Mamaw Honeycutt, she just nodded and wandered outside toward the mimosa tree.

When it got dark, Junior brought Bessie over to stay with Momma. I give Junior my daddy's map with the roads to South Carolina marked.

Junior had loaded the truck with hay. He piled the bales in the truck so that there was a hollow space right behind the cab. We spread a blanket on the floor of the hollow space and climbed in.

Bessie handed me a brown paper sack. "I don't want y'all going hungry. Here's some cornbread with blackberry jelly." Then she give us two bottles of root beer. "Just in case you get thirsty," she said. "But there's only two, so you'll have to share."

"What if I have to pee?" asked Ida.

Junior said, "Just reach up and knock on the back window. I'll stop just as quick as I can." Then he pulled a canvas over the load of hay and tied it down with some rope. We pulled in our heads just in time for him to tie the last of the canvas.

It was dark in there and stuffy too, but at least it was soft. Ida and Ellie wanted to drink the root beer and eat the cornbread before we was even off the dirt road. But I made them wait. "First we have to play 'I'm Going to South Carolina,'" I said. "You have to name what you're going to take with you, starting with the letter *A* and going all the way to *Z*. When we get to the end, we'll each have a piece of cornbread and open one of them drinks."

It wasn't that far to the state line—less than two hours—but I didn't have no way of knowing when we'd get there. The girls got tired of being in the dark hole, and Ida decided about thirty minutes down the road that she had to pee.

"I told you to go before we left," I said.

"I did. But I got to go again."

"Well, you'll just have to wait. We can't be stopping every half hour on account of Mamaw and Papaw are expecting us at eleven thirty."

Finally, when I got tired of Ida holding herself and wiggling, I reached up and tapped on the window. "We have to wait till Junior finds the right place to stop," I said to Ida. "There can't be any cars around. And you're gonna have to go in the bushes because we're staying away from gas stations and diners."

It took Junior another fifteen minutes or so to pull over to the side of the road. When he pulled back the canvas, we nearly trampled each other to be the first one out. But then Ellie was scared to go into the woods. She wanted that blanket, so Junior got it and wrapped it around her shoulders.

Junior headed for one side of the road and we went to the other. There was a tall pine woods on both sides with lots of bushes to hide behind. I told Ida and Ellie to pretend they was going into Wisteria Mansion.

We was barely finished doing our business when I seen headlights through the bushes and heard a car slowing down. And then I seen a red light come on at the front of the car and knew it was the police.

I heard voices. I couldn't hear everything they said, but Junior was loud and I heard him explaining that he was just taking a rest stop. Then I heard something about hay, and I could tell he was showing his load to whoever it was. I was so scared I think I stopped breathing. What if the police found the hollow space where we was hiding? Would he come looking for us? Would I be in trouble for smuggling my sisters out of polio country?

I had my hands tight over Ida's and Ellie's mouths. "Don't make a noise," I whispered. "If they catch us you can't go to Mamaw Honeycutt's." As soon as I said it I just knew the police heard me. It's scary how loud a whisper can be. I sucked in my breath and waited.

I could tell the policeman was moving the hay around in the back of the truck. Was he looking for us?

Ellie whimpered, and I smashed her face into my belly so he wouldn't hear her.

Next thing I knew, I heard Daddy's truck cranking up, and just like that, Junior and the police car took off and left us there. There we were—stuck in the middle of nowheres in the dead of the night with nothing but a blanket. The girls started squalling, and I wanted to bawl too, but I didn't because it was my job to act tough.

"Don't worry," I said. "Junior'll be back, first chance he gets."

I did some hard praying then for sure.

I told Ellie she was a smart girl to bring that blanket to wrap up in. "Why, I bet that police didn't once think there was three girls hiding in the woods. But if he seen that blanket in the back of the truck, he'd be suspicious for sure."

We got a laugh just thinking how we fooled that police.

But we didn't laugh for long because the girls got scared, and to be honest, I wasn't feeling so safe myself. So I made up stories about Wisteria Mansion to keep our minds off all the bad things that could happen to us in that dark woods.

After a while we heard a car come down the road so slow it practically stopped. I didn't see no lights flashing, but I just knew it was the police snooping around. It went on by and before long it come back again the other way. It went like that—two or three more times, back and forth.

"Maybe it's Junior," said Ellie after it went by the second time. "Maybe he can't find us."

"No, it ain't Junior," I said. "Daddy's truck don't sound like that."

"I want Junior to come," whimpered Ida.

"Not now you don't," I whispered. "If he comes when that police is nosing around here, we're gonna be in trouble."

Ida's whimpering turned into crying.

"Stop crying," I said. "That ain't going to fix a thing. Pray for that police to go away and Junior to come back after that."

"I can't pray," said Ida. "I'm too scared."

I wrapped that blanket tight as a cocoon around both of them and made them sit on a log. "Well then," I said, "just say, 'Lord, have mercy.' That's what Bessie says, and it works for everything."

So we all said it together, over and over. "Lord, have mercy. Lord, have mercy."

The police didn't come no more after the fourth time, but it seemed like a long wait before Junior finally come. I held my breath when I seen headlights slowing down again. But then I heard it was Daddy's truck and then Junior whistled

Bob-white. I whistled back—*Bob-bob-white.* And then all three of us went running for that truck.

When Junior seen us, he said, "Ann Fay Honeycutt, you're gonna be the death of me yet. That police thought I was running moonshine. Of course, he didn't find nothing but an empty sack and a couple of bottles that smelled like root beer. It's hard telling what he thought I'd been up to in the back of that truck."

Junior fussed at me the whole time he was shifting those hay bales around and tying that canvas overtop of us.

"Well, he was snooping around," I said. "You better hurry up and get out of here before he comes back."

Junior kept right on telling me about his adventure. "I had to keep driving until he stopped tailing me and then I had to find another way back. Your grandpa will have the state patrol looking for us," he said. "We ain't never gonna make it to that schoolhouse by eleven thirty."

And we didn't either. It was way past midnight by the time we got to where we was supposed to meet Mamaw and Papaw. Ellie and Ida was both asleep, but they woke up when Papaw tickled their noses with hay. He lifted them over the side of the truck and put them in Mamaw's big hug.

Papaw give me a squeeze that nearly took my breath away. Then he pulled a dollar bill out of his pocket and put it in my hand. "Spend it on yourself," he said. "Go see a picture show and buy yourself a trinket. You been working too hard." He put his hand under my chin and lifted my head. "I know you promised your daddy to take care of things. Well, you can quit worrying about these girls. Your mamaw will spoil them rotten even before we get to Georgia."

Then Mamaw gave me a big hug and said, "Oh, Susie Q,

I wish I could take you with me." For as long as I can remember, Susie Q has been Mamaw's pet name for me. Just hearing her say it made me wish I could go home with her instead of back to my momma.

Papaw give Junior a big handshake and I seen him slip some money in his hand. "You're a fine young man," he said. "And I pray this war is over before you turn eighteen and get drafted."

On the way home I sat up front with Junior. I leaned into the door on my side of the truck and put my feet on the seat between us. By the light of the dashboard I seen the outline of his face. He looked strong and manly, and it put a home-sickness in me for my daddy. I sat and stared at him, wishing my staring could turn him into Daddy. I was so tired. I just wanted the war and polio and everything hard to go away.

Junior looked tired too, and it hit me what all I had put him through that night.

"Junior," I said, "I reckon you never knew what you was getting into when you told Daddy you'd take care of us."

"I reckon I didn't," he said.

"Well, I thank you for everything you do for us. Nobody could take the place of Daddy. But you're the next best thing and I don't know what I'd do without you."

16

Tough as Hickory
September 1944

Once I got it in my head to get that wisteria away from the garden, nothing would stop me. I got every tool I could find—Momma's biggest butcher knife, Daddy's handsaw, and his scythe. I marched down past the garden with them tools, dragging a shovel behind me.

I started hacking with the butcher knife. When I got to where it was rooted into Daddy's ditch, I dug it out with the shovel. I used all of those tools to chop, cut, saw, and dig that vine out of my garden.

And I noticed something when I did. The handle on every tool was made of the same thing—hickory wood. I knew it by its straight grain. And my daddy had told me tool handles are made of hickory because it don't break easy. Same as he told me Roosevelt was tough as hickory.

For some reason, that hickory wood give me the gumption to do that job. I told myself I was tough as President Roosevelt and a hickory nut tree put together. I didn't care how many blisters I got or how wet with sweat my overalls was—I was fixing to lick that vine!

But I had other work to do too. The dirty clothes was piling up in the washtubs on the back porch. I would've put them off until the next day, but Peggy Sue's mother was actually planning to take us to the picture show again. I knew she was still nervous about polio, but I wasn't about to miss my chance.

After I cut the wisteria back about six feet past the ditch and had it all pulled out of the cherry tree, I put my tools away and started cranking the water bucket down into the well. I used the first bucket to pour over my head.

The water was so cold I went from sweating one minute to shivering the next. I stripped off my overalls and shirt and used a washrag to scrub myself. The muddy water sent little red rivers dripping off my elbows and running down my body.

When I was cooled off and cleaned up, I cranked up more than twenty buckets of water to put into Momma's wringer washer and rinse tubs. About halfway through, I thought my back couldn't take no more. It started to aching and I felt like an old woman all of a sudden. My legs ached too.

I sat down on the porch floor and drunk a big dipper of cold water and told myself to get up and be tough. Me and Momma put some of the water into big kettles to boil on the stove so the whites would come clean.

Finally we plugged up the washer and turned it on.

It took us the rest of the day to wash them clothes and run them through the wringer and the rinse tubs. Momma hung them on the wash line.

She didn't snap the wrinkles as hard as she always done. But she hung everything up in her same old particular way. Largest to smallest with the seams turned back. Underwear on the back row where people going down the road wouldn't see it—even though no one ever goes down our road. And every pair of socks matched up like twin sisters. She always had a pride about how she done her laundry, and I figured if any job would keep her going it was washing clothes.

When the wash was all done but the folding, we ate some potatoes and fried okra.

I was planning to read the newspaper to Momma while she folded the clothes.

But by the time I sat down to read, I felt like an old woman for sure. There was a hard hurting in my back and the tops of my legs. And my left leg felt heavy as a sledge-hammer.

"I knew that wisteria was going to be the death of me," I said. "And now I'm so stiff I can't hardly move."

Momma give me a worried look and put down the pair of socks she was folding in to itself. She come to where I stood and put her hand on my head. "You're warm," she said. I seen the worry wrinkles on her forehead.

"Oh, I'm not sick—just tired, that's all. I'll just read the paper and then I'll go to bed." I sunk down on the sofa and opened the paper. First I read a few stories on the front page about the war.

I didn't read the latest news about the polio hospital because I never knew how Momma was going to take it. So I started turning the pages to find *Hometown Girl*. But it felt like every page was a whole book. My fingers couldn't hardly do the job.

Somehow I found the page and started reading the story, but then my head started to hurt. It hurt so bad I didn't even want to read. But I was determined because I knew I had got Momma interested.

Of course she could've read it for herself, but I had got so used to taking care of her, I didn't even think about that. I just kept on reading until the words started sliding out of my sight. At first I didn't know what was happening, but then I seen that the paper had slid right out of my hands.

I felt it slide down my leg and onto the floor, and I heard the words I was reading slip off into a whisper. My momma was overtop of me then, shaking me and fanning me with the paper. She brought a wet cloth and put it on my head and another one on my neck and chest, and it felt like the coldest thing I could think of. It felt like Bobby's skin on the day we buried him.

I tried to push the cold cloth off, but I couldn't lift a finger. Momma said, "Ann Fay, see if you can put your head to your chest." I didn't know why she was saying it, but I tried. I just couldn't do it. I felt her tears dropping on my face, and I heard her saying, "Oh no, not you too. Not my baby girl."

I never knew Momma thought of me as her baby until I heard her say it. But when I did, I give up trying to be tough. I didn't worry about overalls and responsibility or hickory wood. I just laid helpless on the couch and let my momma take care of me.

She said she was going after Junior and the truck and we was going to the emergency hospital.

And then she was gone, and I was there staring at the ceiling. A fly was walking across it, and I thought how that fly might be the one that brought polio back to our house.

I prayed for my legs to move and Junior to come quick.

Well, this was one time when Junior didn't come running. Him and Bessie must've been visiting some neighbors. Momma told me she couldn't find them anywhere, so she took Daddy's truck, which was sitting in the yard. My momma can't drive no more than I can—not as good even, because at least Daddy would let me sit on his lap and steer sometimes or help him shift the gears. But Momma never even tried to drive.

Well, like I told Junior, where there's a will, there's a way, and my momma had the will to take me to that hospital. She picked me up and carried me out to the truck and laid me in the front seat. "My baby girl is not riding to the hospital in a hearse," she said.

Every move she made hurt me. But I knew she was doing her best to take care of me, so I tried not to cry out. She climbed in the truck and put my feet up on her lap and drove off.

It was a bumpy ride because she wasn't good at shifting them gears. Every jerk felt like it was slamming my body against a rock chimney. I know I moaned and cried because I remember my momma saying, "I'm sorry, girl baby. I'm sorry. But I'm not letting you go to that hospital in a hearse. We're almost there. It'll only be another minute."

It wasn't another minute. It was maybe thirty minutes to the hospital. My momma jerked and stalled that truck and started it up again at every stop sign. The whole time, she was praying, "Oh, Lord God, dear Jesus, please don't take my baby girl. She's all I got now."

I felt bad then for taking the twins away from her, so I tried to tell her they was coming home soon. I tried to tell her Daddy was coming home from the war too, but I didn't believe it. And I couldn't get no words out. My head felt like it was splitting wide open.

So I give up trying to talk. I just listened to her pray. "Please don't take my baby girl. She's just a little baby girl."

And I reckon that's what I was, on account of not long after I got to the hospital they put me in a diaper.

17

Colored Girl
September 1944

They got me out of the truck and put me on a cot, quick as
my momma jerked to a stop. They took me into a tent with
a screen door and a sign on the outside that said ADMISSION
TENT.

I thought them doctors and nurses was trying their best
to torture me. I squeezed Momma's hand while the doctor
stuck a needle in my back.

"Hush, honey," I heard my momma say whenever I cried
out. "It's gonna be all right." But I could tell from the sound
of her voice that she was scared. Somehow it made me feel
better, hearing her worry over me for a change.

While I laid there and suffered, it hit me that God was
punishing me for working Bobby till he dropped. I was the
cause of him dying. I told myself that whatever them doctors done to me wouldn't be bad enough to pay for what I
done to Bobby.

Just when I felt like I got Momma back, they took her
away. I heard them telling her to go home because the health
officer would be coming out to see her in the morning. I
knew right then Momma was going to burn every little
thing of mine just like I done with Bobby's.

I heard Momma worrying over them putting me in an
iron lung. But the doctors told her I didn't appear to have

that kind of polio. I didn't want Momma to leave me, but I didn't complain because I wasn't a tiny boy like Bobby. I was the man of the house, and I had to face this like a man.

They took off all my clothes and put me in a little diaper-looking thing with strings to untie it on the sides. And they put a halter on my top. I like to died of embarrassment. Here I was with hardly a stitch on and all kinds of doctors poking me all over. But I reckoned it was part of my punishment, so I didn't argue. I closed my eyes and tried to keep the tears from leaking out the edges.

They finally give me a gown and put me to bed in another place, but I was so sad and tired and my legs hurt so bad I didn't pay no attention to where I was. A nurse with a white mask was rubbing my legs real gentle, but even that hurt me so bad it took my breath away. So she just held my hand and sung "When the Lights Go On Again." It was comforting to hear her singing about the end of the war, even if it did sound a little strange through that mask.

When she started in singing, her song was all mixed up with a noise like something crawling on the outside of a tent I was in. Then I heard where the tent started to rip and a wisteria vine poked itself through the hole and curled itself around the poles that held up the tent. It climbed down those poles and started coming right toward me.

I knew all I had to do was get in my daddy's truck and leave so it wouldn't grow itself around me. But my legs wouldn't move. "Daddy!" I screamed. "It's fixing to choke the life out of me. Help!"

I seen my daddy then, but there was an ocean between us. He started toward me, walking on water. But the wisteria sucked up all the water and wrapped itself around my daddy. Then it wrapped itself all around me too. We was wrapped up like two caterpillars in the same sweet-smelling cocoon. And my daddy kept saying, "Don't worry, Ann Fay. When we get outta this dark place, we're gonna fly."

I tried to kick my way out, but my legs wouldn't move. It seemed like I struggled for days to get free of it.

Then all of a sudden I seen a bright light off in the distance. I reached out for it. I pushed my heavy eyelids open and it was broad daylight. I was staring at the ceiling and it was a tent for sure, but it didn't have no holes in it and there wasn't no wisteria in sight. I knew then it was a nightmare I had.

I started looking around and seen that the tent was mostly just the roof of that place I was in. There was a wood floor and wood going about four feet up the walls. On top of that was a window screen that went up to the tent ceiling. And there was flaps rolled up that could be let down in case of rain. I seen there was about twenty beds in that one tent room. I turned my head to the right and was never so shocked in all my born days.

Right there in the bed beside me—not three feet away— was a colored girl. And her big eyes was staring right at me.

I jerked my head away real fast, and when I did, I heard her snicker. I reckon she got some pleasure out of surprising me like that.

I knew from the newspapers that the polio hospital took coloreds, but it never crossed my mind that they would put them side by side with white people.

Then the colored girl started talking. "You were sure enough out of your head when they brung you in," she said. "I thought they had gave me a crazy white girl for a neighbor."

BLUE

I didn't like her calling me crazy. So I didn't give her the satisfaction of an answer.

After she seen I wasn't going to say nothing, she spoke up again. "Then I got to figuring it was just the fever making you holler out like that," she said. "I had it real bad too, at first. I was burning up so bad I was calling for the fire department."

I waited a spell and then I snuck a peek at the colored girl. When I did, she was still staring. So I stared back at her. But she kept her eyes right on me.

"Hey," she said. "My name is Imogene Wilfong. What's yourn?"

I reckon she thought we was going to be friends. But I hadn't ever been that close to a colored before. I sure hadn't thought about making friends with one. Instead of telling her my name, I looked away.

Next thing I knew, a nurse come to my bed with pieces of dark wool cloth. She wrapped it around my legs like she was measuring them with it. Then she started cutting it.

"I'm getting your Kenny pack ready," she said.

I remembered reading about Kenny packs in the papers. I knew they was made of army blankets, but I didn't have no idea who Kenny was or how an army blanket could help polio.

"Who's Kenny?" I asked. "And how does his packs make you feel better?"

Imogene snickered. "Miss Emma, tell her who Kenny is."

The nurse said, "Sister Elizabeth Kenny. She was an army nurse in Australia who found a better way to treat polio. If it weren't for her, the doctors would be putting your legs in splints. Or your whole body in a cast. But the children they did that to—well, they just froze up that way and never got better. Thanks to Sister Kenny, you'll probably learn to walk again."

Miss Emma slipped a piece of that wool under my backside, wrapped it around the front of me, and pulled it tight before she cut it to size.

"That stuff itches," I said.

But Miss Emma didn't pay me no mind. She just kept right on explaining. "Sister Kenny is in the United States now, teaching her methods to polio specialists. She says muscles need to be limber. So we heat the wool and wrap it around the parts of you that polio has affected. The heat relaxes your muscles and gets them ready for therapy."

Imogene snickered again, and I didn't think it was because the nurse's voice sounded funny behind her mask. It was more like she knew some secret the nurse had forgot to tell me. Seemed like that girl had plenty to snicker about.

It wasn't long till the nurses got real busy with Kenny packs. They rolled in big silver pots on stands with wheels. You should've seen the steam coming out of them pots. The nurse pulled a piece of wet cloth out of the pot and it was steaming too. She waved it in the air a little and said, "Now just relax and let the heat do its work."

Then she started wrapping the hot cloth around my leg. I was so shocked I screamed right out. "Stop!" I hollered. "You're scalding me!"

"I'm sorry, honey," she said. "I have to do this. We put them through a wringer to get the extra water out. So it's not going to burn you. But I have to do this. It'll make you feel better."

She put them on both my legs. And on my left arm and my hips and belly too. I tried to kick them off, but my legs wouldn't kick. I shrunk away as best I could, and moaned.

Then somehow, through all my moaning, I heard a voice beside me.

"It mostly hurts at first," the voice said. "After a while it starts to feel better." And then I heard it again. "It mostly hurts at first. After a while it starts to feel better."

Over and over like a momma's bedtime song, the voice said it. And somehow it helped me. I laid real still and listened, and I could feel the tears oozing out of the corners of my eyes.

I opened my eyes and stared into Imogene's. They was brownish green and gentle and loving—like a momma's eyes. Her voice was soft and sweet—like a momma's voice. "It mostly hurts at first," she whispered. "After a while it starts to feel better."

I didn't say nothing. I just stared into her eyes to get me some comfort. I pulled up the corner of my sheet and bit it as hard as I could.

The nurse wrapped a layer of rubber and then dry cloth on top of the hot wool and pinned everything in place. Imogene explained. "The rubber keeps the bed from getting wet," she said. "And the cloth holds the heat in."

I laid there and listened and tried not to cry, and then I heard the nurse say, "You're all done for now."

"Oh, boy," said Imogene. "I reckons it's my turn." All of a sudden she was hanging on to her sheet too.

Miss Emma was fixing to put a Kenny pack on her. She waved the wool in the air a little, and I could see the steam leaving it. Then she took the hot wool and started wrapping it around Imogene's chest. I heard Imogene suck in her breath real hard.

"You's killing me, Miss Emma," she said.

Miss Emma just kept on working and Imogene moaned.

BLUE

I could see that hot wool bothered her every bit as much as it did me. I wanted to say something to make her feel better, but I didn't know what to say—except what she said to me. So I said it.

"It mostly hurts at first," I whispered. "After a while it starts to feel better."

Imogene looked at me all surprised-like. "Is you telling me you believed that pack o' lies?" she asked. Then she started to laugh.

I laughed too. I laughed because I knew that it wasn't no lie. I really did feel better. Those wool packs was starting to cool off a little. And not only that, it seemed like the hard pain in my legs and backside was starting to let up.

There was another reason I laughed. I laughed because I had a new friend.

I had got to be friends with a colored girl.

18

The Hospital
September 1944

I found out real quick that polio picked on whoever it took a notion to hit. Some of us was white, and others was colored. Some was rich, but lots of us didn't have a dime to spare.

Now we was all in the same predicament—stuck in a row of hospital beds with no way to get out unless we fell out. Whenever I looked around, I seen girls who was as bad off as I was, or worse. Just like me, they couldn't even walk to the bathroom when they needed to.

And when we used the bedpan, we didn't have no privacy because we was all in one big open ward. But at least all us girls was shamed together. I reckon that's why we become such good friends.

When the Kenny packs got cold, the wool itched worse than a rash of poison ivy. And we couldn't do a thing but lay there and suffer. I laid there in that strong-smelling wet wool every day except Sunday.

After they took the packs off, the physios—that's the physiotherapists—would massage our muscles to limber them up. My physio was Miss Ruth.

She had short brown hair and big brown eyes that was always twinkling. And she wanted me to get well almost as much as I did. I reckon that's why she worked me and my muscles so hard.

BLUE

And another thing—I had to lay with my feet pressed flat against a board at the foot of the bed. It wasn't one bit comfortable.

"That so you don't get drop foot," Imogene said. "Some folks gets it and they feet goes to pointing down and won't never come back right again."

Imogene told me who all the nurses was and where they was from. Seemed like just about every one of them come from someplace else. One even come from California.

Imogene pointed out the convicts to me too. "They was so desperate for help they brung prisoners in here to work," she said. "But don't you worry over it. They just as good as the next person. And some of them is better, for true."

Imogene told me she was from Greensboro. She said she had six brothers and sisters. And her daddy was in the army.

Naturally, I thought back to that day at the train station when I watched my daddy and a colored soldier going off to war at the same time. And all of a sudden I understood something. I understood why I felt like *I* was the one starting out on a journey.

Meeting Imogene was part of that journey.

"I reckon just about everyone's daddy is in the war nowadays," I said.

She said her daddy was at an army camp for coloreds, waiting to be shipped out. "I heard tell of some colored soldiers going overseas," she said. "But my daddy been in the army for more than a year and he ain't been sent out yet."

"Well, then I reckon you know he won't be killed," I said. I told her I would give anything to know my daddy would come home from the war. I told her about the overalls he give me and how he taught me to climb trees and do fractions. How to pray and not give up when things get tough. I told her my daddy always said, *That's my opinion and it's worth two cents.* "But if you ask me," I said, "every word that comes out of my daddy's mouth is pure gold."

I told her about my momma and my twin sisters, but I didn't tell her about Bobby.

I asked a nurse named Hazel when my momma could come see me.

"The doctors sent her home to get some rest," said Nurse Hazel. "She can't see you anyway, as long as you're in the contagious ward. So she might as well take care of the home place."

"I don't think my momma can take care of herself right now," I said. "Much less the home place."

I give Peggy Sue's telephone number to the nurse and asked her would she send a message to Junior to look out for my momma.

The next day Junior called back and told Nurse Hazel that Momma was in good hands.

I said, "Well, I knew I could count on Junior and Bessie."

"That young man said your momma snapped out of her bad spell when she brought you to the hospital," said Nurse Hazel.

Two days later I got a letter from my momma, and sure enough, she sounded like her old self.

Dear Ann Fay,

I wish I could be with you. But the hospital staff insisted I come home. They said the worst of the epidemic is over and they aren't so desperate for help. And I didn't want to ask for a place to stay again. I'll get Junior to bring me to the hospital as soon as they let me see you.

*Junior picked the last of the corn and Bessie helped me
put it in jars.*

*Mamaw Honeycutt sent a letter saying the twins was
down there getting spoiled rotten as a bushel of apples sitting in the sun. I sent your daddy the hospital's address
so he can write you there. A letter from him will be good
medicine for you.*

*I pray for you every day all day long. You have been
such a help since your daddy left. I don't know what I
would do without you.*

All my love,

Momma

Well, that scared me—her saying she didn't know
what she would do without me. Did Momma think I might
die?

I closed my eyes and thought about Bobby. I thought
how he was in here for more than a month before he died.
If he could last that long and still die, maybe I could too. I
hadn't been there even a whole week yet.

I wondered what dying felt like. Did it feel like the sharp
pain in my muscles? Or more like drifting off to sleep? That
night I tried my best to stay awake because I thought maybe
I wouldn't wake up.

Nurse Hazel come around to check on us and seen that I
had my eyes open. "Hey," she said. "Aren't you sleepy tonight?"
She pulled a stool up by my bed and started singing, *"Now I lay
me down to sleep, angels watching over me, my Lord ..."*

I laid there and listened to the whole song. It reminded
me of the bedtime prayer my daddy used to say with me.
It even had that part in there—*"If I die before I wake, angels
watching over me, my Lord. Pray the Lord my soul to take ..."*

BLUE

That done it. I couldn't hold it back no longer. "Am I gonna die?" I asked.

"Oh," she said. "Is that what's keeping you up?" She pulled my sheet up around my shoulders and tucked me in just like my momma used to do. "Honey," she said, "most polio patients don't die. And this hospital hasn't lost many patients at all."

"My brother died," I said. "He was here for over a month before he died."

"I know," she said. "I remember Bobby. But he had two kinds of polio—your kind and the kind that affects the lungs."

All of a sudden I started to cry.

She gripped my arm. "I'm sorry about your brother. I bet you were the best big sister in the world."

"No," I moaned. "I killed him."

"Oh, no, honey. You didn't kill him. He had a bad case of polio."

"But he told me he was sick and I didn't believe him. I made him work in the garden. Then all of a sudden he couldn't move a bit."

"So that's why you think it's your fault," said Nurse Hazel.

"And that ain't all," I said. "On top of all that, I had to burn every last one of his toys and even his picture drawings so the twins wouldn't get polio too. We don't have one single thing to remember him by. Even our dog, Pete, followed him to the hospital and never come back."

"Pete?" asked Nurse Hazel. "Polio Pete was your dog? Oh, my Lord, honey. Of course he couldn't come back. I mean—" She clapped her hand over her mouth like she was keeping something awful from coming out of it.

"What?" I asked. "Do you know where Pete is?"

Nurse Hazel pulled the sheet up around my shoulders and run her hand along my arm. "I'm sorry about your dog," she said.

"Where is he?" I asked. "Tell me! I need to know why Pete never made it home. We was counting on him to come back."

"Oh, honey," said Nurse Hazel. "I don't want to say it." She smoothed the hair away from my forehead and tucked it behind my ears. "Pete disappeared from the hospital a few weeks ago. At first we thought someone stole him. But then one day we found him. He had crawled way back under the hospital."

Nurse Hazel's voice got real slow and whispery then— like a mystery was showing itself to her. "Somehow Pete must have known about Bobby," she said. "I guess your Pete died of a broken heart."

Then she put her head down on my arm. I think she was crying, only she didn't want me to see it. But it was a comfort to me just knowing Nurse Hazel loved my brother and his dog. I reckon I fell asleep with her patting my arm. At least I don't remember her getting up and leaving.

19

The Bottle Collection
September 1944

The next morning Imogene must have woke up before the breakfast cooks got out of bed. My eyes wasn't open long enough to get the blurry out before I heard her talking.

"Why didn't you tell me about your brother?" she demanded.

Who did Imogene Wilfong think she was, anyway? If I could've rolled over and turned my back on her, I would have. Was I supposed to tell her every little thing about my life just because I got stuck in a hospital beside her?

She lay there under that white sheet, flat on her back with her feet poking up against the footboard and only her head sticking out, all full of wisdom. "Your brother dying of polio ain't no little thing," she said.

"Well, maybe that's why I didn't tell you."

"Don't you know when something hurts that bad you got to tell somebody. You don't want to bust wide open, do you?"

That's what it felt like. Like the guilt was filling me up and looking for a way to bust loose. I didn't say nothing for a long time. But finally I said, "Well, now you know. My brother died and it was all my fault."

Thank goodness the volunteers come in then with our breakfast. They saved me from having to talk about Bobby.

But Imogene can be downright nosey when she wants to. Oh, she let me alone for a while—till after our cereal was gone and the nurses put on our Kenny packs. Then she brought it up again.

"It's not your fault about your brother."

Something about Imogene—I can't ignore her for long. "You're just like my neighbor, Junior Bledsoe," I said. "Thinking you know everything."

"Well, answer me this—where was your momma when your brother got polio?"

"At home, cooking and cleaning and washing."

"Right there with you and your brother and sisters? Right there when you was working him in the garden? How come she didn't pick that child up and put him in his bed and make him sleep?"

"'Cause he didn't seem like he was sick. He had a cold at first, but then it seemed like he was over it."

"And where was your momma when *you* got sick?"

"At home. Helping me when she could keep her mind on it."

"And did she put you to bed? Did she tell you to go lay down and stop working your daddy's garden?"

"My momma didn't know I was sick. To tell you the truth, *I* didn't even know it."

"Well, then—is it her fault you got polio?"

I thought about my momma wandering around the house like a lost child and I knew I couldn't blame her for my misery.

"Just like I thought," said Imogene. "It's not your momma's fault you got polio. It's not her fault your brother got it. It's just yours, ain't it? You the only one who done wrong. And you done it all on purpose, didn't you?"

The way Imogene said it, she almost made sense. But it wasn't that easy for me. I could see us, clear as yesterday—Bobby sitting in the dirt, lifting his chubby little hand full of dust and dropping it on Pete's tail. Telling me he was sick. And me, getting all mad and making him work till he dropped.

"I reckons when your Daddy went off to the war he give you that pair of overalls you told me about so as you could be God while he gone. I reckons stepping into a pair of britches means you gets to decide who lives and who dies."

"Of course not!" I said. "If it was up to me, wouldn't nobody die."

"Well, all right then. So you not a murderer after all."

Between the hot wool and Imogene being such a smart aleck I was feeling real irritable.

"I never said I was a murderer."

"No, but it all your fault. Like you was supposed to know things only God could know."

Since Imogene seemed to know so much about everything, I went ahead and asked her about God Himself. "Do you think God even knows we got polio?" I asked.

Imogene laid there all wise and wonderful with them pieces of army blankets and white cloths wrapped all around her—practically up to her neck. She didn't move a muscle, not even to turn and look at me when she spoke. She just stared at the tent roof and said, "He sees it."

"Maybe He turns His head," I said. "Maybe He can't stand to look."

"Maybe," said Imogene. "But that ain't what my momma say. She say that God looks straight onto our sorrow. And when He sees our suffering, it hurt Him bad."

I thought about that for a while. And just when I noticed

that my hot packs had started to itch me, I heard Imogene say, "Ann Fay, are you telling me you don't know nothing about God's bottle collection?"

"God's bottle collection? Imogene, what in the wide world are you talking about?"

"I thought you go to church."

"I do—every Sunday except when there's an epidemic. But my preacher ain't never said nothing about God's bottle collection."

"Well, maybe white peoples just never needed to know. But my peoples—we have so many tears, we knows all about it from way back."

"Imogene, you're talking nonsense is what you're doing. What does your people's tears got to do with bottles?"

"Well, it's not just for my peoples. I reckons the Bible be for everybody in the world. It say in the book of Psalms that God has put all my tears in His bottle. My momma told me that God has got a whole row of bottles up on His big fine windowsill—one for every one of His childrens. She say when we cries, He catches our tears in His big gentle hands and pours them into our own personal bottle."

When Imogene said that, I started in laughing again. I just couldn't help it. I tried to think how big God's windowsill must be if it could hold a bottle for every one of His children. And I laughed because I liked what I seen in my mind's eye. I seen a whole row of bottles—from here to across the ocean, I reckoned. And every one was a different shape and size. And all colors too. I seen the tears of the whole world in them bottles. And I seen the sun shining up a rainbow on their tears.

And all of a sudden I felt so good I couldn't hardly speak. My heart was so full I wanted to get out of my bed and hug that Imogene. But, of course, I couldn't move. So I just laid there and watched the sun make a sparkly pattern all over her from where it was shining through the tree leaves outside our window.

Imogene seen me staring at her and said, "What? Why you got so quiet?"

"I was wondering," I said. "What color is your bottle?"

"Hmmm," said Imogene. "I reckons I ain't thought about my bottle having a color. What color is yours?"

"How should I know? I didn't even know I had a bottle till just this minute." We both started laughing again. Then I said, "Well, how about I pick you a color and you pick me one."

So that's what we done.

When I thought about choosing a bottle for Imogene, I thought right off about a vase that Mamaw Honeycutt keeps in her corner cupboard. It's made of carnival glass and it's sort of light brown with rainbow colors bouncing off it. You can't see through carnival glass. So when I imagined it sitting on God's windowsill, I couldn't see how full of tears her bottle was. But that seemed right to me, because I didn't know nothing about the troubles her people seen. But I knew God could see right through that glass. He could see every tear.

Then Imogene said my bottle had to be blue—like them overalls my daddy give me. Like the sky above. Like the color of truth and faithfulness—because that's how I was. When she said that, I cried all over again.

And this time I knew my tears wasn't soaking into my bedsheets. My tears was rolling right into the hand of God.

20

Imogene's People

October 1944

Peggy Sue wrote to me at the hospital, and I let Imogene read the letter. I told her how Peggy Sue's mother took us to the picture show sometimes on Saturday afternoon. Before the epidemic made her nervous, anyway.

"Maybe when we get out of here, you can go too," I said.

Well, you should've seen the look Imogene give me then. First her mouth dropped open so wide I could've stuck my arm—Kenny pack and all—right in it. Then she busted out laughing.

"What's so funny?" I asked.

"The polio done gone to your head," said Imogene. "Has your Peggy Sue even seen the whites of a colored girl's eyes? And what about her momma? How many coloreds has she carried in her fine car?"

"At least one," I said. "They have a colored maid."

"Well, I reckons anyone who has a colored woman washing her floors ain't likely to let her girl go to the picture show with me."

"Hey," I said. "Mrs. Rhinehart is a Christian woman."

"Oh," said Imogene. "Well, I reckons that changes everything. So just supposing she and her little girl thinks it's a wonderful idea. When we gets to the picture house, which door we gonna use?"

"Huh?"

"Is you going in the back door, up them rickety steps to the balcony? 'Cause I can't go in the front door. And where we gonna sit?"

"Oh," I said. I knew the colored folks always sat up in the balcony. But for a little bit there, I almost forgot how things was outside the hospital.

"That's okay," said Imogene. "My momma wouldn't let me go with you to the movie house anyhow."

"Why?" I asked.

Imogene looked at me like I had lost my mind. "Don't forget. You white."

"Yeah?"

"My momma say she ain't never met a white person she could trust."

"That's not very nice," I said.

"And that's what my momma say about white peoples. They not very nice."

"Maybe your momma ain't seen the whites of our eyes neither. Maybe she thinks all white people are like the slave owners. But that was a long time ago."

"Maybe," said Imogene. "Or maybe it's because she can't hardly visit her momma in South Carolina because she can't find a place to use the bathroom along the way. Maybe it's because her childrens have to ride over an hour on the schoolbus and drive past three white schools getting there. I hope you know there's a muddy wide river between your people and mines."

I ain't never thought about the way coloreds had to do before. But I still thought it was wrong of Imogene's momma not to trust some white people.

"Well," I said, "it's just a few white people that makes

them decisions. Most of us are not like that."

"I know you right," said Imogene. But by the sound of her voice, I knew she didn't mean it. I was feeling put out with her just then.

"Tell me something, Imogene Wilfong," I said. "If you and your momma think white people are so bad, how come you're my friend?"

Imogene thought about that question for a minute. "Well, Ann Fay, it's like this. My momma don't have to be friends with white folks if she don't want to. She got plenty of coloreds to turn to. But when they brung me in this hospital, they wasn't nobody but whites all around me. I know there's other coloreds here, but I don't see none in contagious, do you? What was I gonna do—lay here and keep my mouth shut or make me a friend?" She laughed. "I know you not colored, but you right there beside me, so I reckons you the next best thing."

21

The Muddy Wide River
October 1944

I reckon me and Imogene would never've been friends if we hadn't got stuck with each other. But it didn't take long for either one of us to be glad we did.

There was other girls all around us, and we played guessing games with them and told stories to pass the time of day. But it was different with Imogene. I got to know her in a way I never did know the other girls. I got to know her fighting spirit that wouldn't let me get by with thinking the way I used to about things—especially about coloreds. And I learned lots of little secrets about her life because we kept each other awake at night, talking and giggling after the lights was out.

We both knew we was going to be in that hospital for a long time—months and months, maybe. And we wasn't one bit sad about spending them months together.

Then one day some hospital helpers come to get me and Imogene and a few other girls.

"Good news," said one of the helpers. "They're letting you out of contagious. Ready, set, go!" And just like that, they started gathering us up and getting us disinfected for the move. They took Imogene out first and pushed me right behind her.

We had to go outside and down a long wooden ramp to get to our new ward. The minute we was outside I felt like

I was home. The sound of birds singing and the smell of the pine trees washed right over me. "Oh," I begged, "please let us stay out here."

"Well," said the helper, "now that you're out of contagious, you can go outside sometimes for sunshine. But right now we need to get you settled in your new home."

I laid on my bed and drunk in the sight of the tall pines overhead. The pine needles made a lacy curtain between me and the sky. A bird whistled and I said hello back to him.

I watched the volunteers that was pushing Imogene's bed. They was heading for the rock building—it was the camp building from before this place was a hospital. I started thinking how me and Imogene was gonna feel downright rich in that place.

But then the people that was pushing my bed started up a different ramp, into a new ward that was just barely built. "Stop!" I said. And they did stop. That is, the ones that was pushing my bed stopped. But them that was pushing Imogene just kept right on going.

"Imogene!" I hollered. "Stop!" I seen Imogene turn then, and her eyes and mouth went into big circles when she seen they was putting us in different places.

"Ann Fay!" she called, and I seen on her confused face everything I was feeling in my heart.

The volunteers that was moving Imogene slowed down for a minute and looked at me. They seen our arms reaching out to each other, one black and one white, but they just shook their heads and started pushing her bed again— pushing it away from me.

The volunteers that was moving my bed started pushing again too. And the blond woman explained. "When you leave contagious, Negroes and whites have separate wards."

For the last couple of weeks, me and Imogene was looking forward to getting out of contagious, and nobody ever said, "You won't see each other after that." And it never crossed my mind that my bed wouldn't be right beside Imogene's the whole time I was in that hospital.

"No!" I said. "I want to go where Imogene's going."

The volunteer at the foot of my bed stopped and put her hands on her big hips. She squinted those green eyes and shook that head with its tight red curls like she knew what I wanted better than I did. "No, you don't," she said and the sound of her voice made me think Imogene was going someplace dreadful.

"But why?" I moaned. It was just like the warm sun and the pine trees and the birds disappeared off the face of the earth. All I seen was the metal bars at the head of Imogene's bed and a big wide volunteer blocking her from my view. All I felt was a bumpy ride up that ramp. I heard Imogene's bed bumping up another ramp, going in another direction.

I didn't pay no mind to where they put me in the new ward or who was in the bed next to me. I didn't want to find out. But I knew for sure she was a white girl.

I laid back on my bed and cried till the tears run off the side of my face and dripped into my ears and back out again. I told myself God was catching them tears for His blue Ann Fay Honeycutt bottle. But with Imogene gone, it was harder for me to believe.

At suppertime, my new nurse—her name was Amanda— set the food tray on the table beside my bed. "Believe me, honey, it's better this way," she said. "Whites and coloreds aren't supposed to share the same hospital. It's just that with the epidemic, they didn't have any choice but to put you together."

Well, it seemed to me like that emergency hospital was

BLUE

doing things the way the world ought to be. How come when there was an emergency they could break all the rules? And when things got better, why did they have to go and put things back in the same old mess the world was in before?

I asked Nurse Amanda was they going to take Imogene to another hospital.

"Oh, no," she said. "Most hospitals don't take polio patients or coloreds. This hospital is very unusual. But don't worry. Imogene is in Ward Eleven. She'll be better off there, with her own kind."

"Well, I'm her kind," I said. "Why don't you take me to Ward Eleven?"

Nurse Amanda looked downright shocked when I said that. She shook her finger at me like I was a naughty child and said, "Stop feeling sorry for yourself and eat your dinner."

That was easy for her to say. She hadn't been in contagious with us. She might not know whites and coloreds could get along. The longer I laid there, the madder I got. And the madder I got, the more I wanted to do something about it.

I didn't have no idea what to do until they brought me the *Hickory Daily Record,* which I had been reading every day, same as before I come to the hospital. That's when I got the idea about writing a letter to the Open Forum section of the paper. I seen how other people wrote letters and complained about things they thought was wrong in the community.

So I asked for a paper and pencil. I wrote:

Dear Editor,
   I'm writing from the emergency polio hospital. When I got here, I was surprised to see a colored girl in the bed

*beside mine. Well, I soon learned that she was not only a
nice girl, but also a lot like me. But when it was time to leave
the contagious ward they put us in different places—her
with Negroes and me with whites.*

*People say it's better for people to stick with their own
kind. But polio showed me that whites and coloreds can live
together in this world. I hope you can do something about
this because me and her already begged and cried and it
didn't do one bit of good.*

Yours truly,
Ann Fay Honeycutt

Nurse Amanda mailed it for me, but she told me I was
wasting my time. I reckon I thought the editor would at
least take the time to write me back. But he didn't. I seen
my letter in the paper about a week after that, and I asked
the nurse would she please take it to Imogene so she could
read it too.

From then on, me and Imogene started writing letters
back and forth. It wasn't as good as having her there beside
me. But it was something to look forward to each day. The
nurses said they was losing weight running back and forth
with our mail.

I'll say one thing for the nurses at that hospital—they
would do just about anything for their patients.

Imogene wrote that they moved her with the other coloreds to a ward in the basement of the rock building. She
said it was cool and damp and she hated it.

I wrote back and said that now I knew what she was
talking about before—about how her people was treated.
I told her when I got out of that hospital I was going to do
something about it.

Then one day she wrote and said water was leaking into the basement. The next day she said they moved all the coloreds to a better ward.

"Well," I said, "at least somebody has got a little bit of decency about them." But I would've felt a lot better if they moved her back with me.

22

Visiting Day
October 1944

Once I was out of contagious, my physio started doing muscle training with me. Every day she'd put me in a big metal tub of warm water, and then she'd exercise my arms and legs and bend my fingers and toes and everything else that would bend. Afterwards, just when I was relaxed and lazy, she'd expect me to work.

She'd stand at the side of my bed and take my left arm. "Concentrate on this muscle," she'd say, giving my arm a little squeeze. "Think hard that it's going to move. I'm the one that's going to move it, but you have to tell it to move. That way we'll train your mind and your muscles to work together again."

So I told my muscle to move my arm, but I knew my mind didn't have nothing to do with it. It was Miss Ruth doing all the moving. But still, she wouldn't let up on me. She made me focus. And after maybe a week or more, I realized I was actually moving my arm! Miss Ruth kept adding other muscles for me to work on. She was a slave driver for sure.

The good thing about being out of contagious was my momma could visit. She came on a warm, sunny day, so the hospital volunteer pushed my bed out to the porch. And that, by itself, was as good as Christmas.

Junior drove Momma to the hospital, so he come along in

for the visit. I think it was the first time I ever seen Junior when he couldn't think of nothing to say. He just sat on the porch floor and waited while me and Momma visited. As much as Junior's talking always bothered me, him looking away from me and being quiet like that bothered me even more.

Momma sat on a wooden chair by my bed. She stroked my arms and said she knew I would walk again. I closed my eyes and tried to feel every little touch of Momma's fingers. She rubbed my arms, and if I sucked my breath in from the pain, she slowed up and said, "Oh, honey, I'm sorry. I never meant to hurt you."

Her voice was so full of tenderness that I felt the tears coming up in my eyes. I tried to hold them back, but a sharp pain come up in my throat when I did. And the tears seemed like they just wanted to come. So I finally give up and let them.

When Momma seen I was crying, she stopped rubbing my arms and started in to singing. *"I come to the garden alone, while the dew is still on the roses ..."*

I reckon my momma knew a garden song would comfort me. Hearing her sing it took me back home again. Laying there with my eyes shut, I could almost pretend Momma was fussing over her roses by the front steps and I was in the vegetable garden trailing behind Daddy. I could almost believe Ida and Ellie was begging Momma for roses to pin in their hair and Bobby was making Pete dizzy in the tire swing.

For a minute or two, Momma's singing put the whole family back together again.

But then the song was finished, and she started telling me how our garden was all done. Only the sweet potatoes needed to be dug and put in the cellar.

I made myself open my eyes. I looked at the pine trees over the emergency hospital and I told myself the truth.

Our family was not home in one piece. Daddy was overseas and Bobby was in his grave. Even Pete was dead.

I told Momma about Imogene. I seen the wrinkles come on her forehead when I told her Imogene was colored. But I went ahead and asked could me and Imogene see each other after we was out of the hospital.

She just said, "That's a bridge we'll have to cross when we get to it."

She took a letter from Daddy out of her pocketbook.

My dear family,

It breaks my heart to know you're suffering there without me. I'm suffering here too, knowing I'll never hold my boy again. I just keep telling myself he's in a better place. At least he'll never have to go to war. Ever since I got to this place one song keeps running in my head.

Precious Lord, take my hand,
Lead me on, help me stand.

Some days I can't believe the Lord would hold my hand in the middle of a war like this. So much killing he would have to walk through.

Ida and Ellie, be good and help your momma and your sister. Ann Fay, I thank you for all you do to help Momma. Don't wear them overalls out before I get home. Myrtle, I'm praying for the day I can be home in your arms. The good Lord willing, it will be soon. The Allied army is taking Europe back from Hitler. Pray it all ends quick.

I pray every night that God will help you with the heavy load you have to bear.

All my love,
Daddy

BLUE

His letter almost made me cry again. I folded it carefully and said, "Daddy don't even know I'm in the hospital, does he?"

Momma sighed and said, "By now he should have my letter. I sent him your address."

After Momma kissed me goodbye and headed for home, I wrote a letter to Daddy.

Dear Daddy,

I know Momma told you I'm at the polio hospital. I kept up the garden as long as I could, but when my muscles stopped working, Momma brought me here. Sometimes I wonder if I'll ever walk again, but Dr. Hahn says I will if I work hard and cooperate with the physios.

At first, polio hurt a lot. But it's getting better. Now the hardest part is laying in bed. Sometimes I feel like a lightning bug in a canning jar. Like if I don't get out of this bed soon, my light is going to burn right out.

They put hot packs on me every day. That's to limber up my muscles. And they put me in tubs of warm water for the same reason. And physios work on my muscles. I can tell they're getting better.

I have good friends here. Especially one named Imogene, who is colored. We want to see each other after we get out of the hospital. Would you take me to see her in Greensboro once you get home from the war?

Daddy, I can't wait for you to come home. I love you better than iced tea with sugar in it.

Love from your spitting image,
Ann Fay

It seemed like it took forever for Daddy's answer to come to me.

Dear Ann Fay,

Oh my little darling, I can't believe you have polio. I feel like it's all my fault because I left you with all the hard work. I should be at home taking care of my family instead of over here fighting this horrible war.

The longer I fight, the worse I hate it. I know someone has to keep the dictators from overtaking the world, but I just don't have the heart for killing my fellow men.

About seeing your friend Imogene after you get out of the hospital—well, I don't know about that. It's best for people to stick with their own kind. When you get out you will have your own friends. What do you hear from Peggy Sue?

Ann Fay, I pray every day for you to walk again soon. All my love,
Daddy

My heart sunk to my toes when I read that about Imogene. It was the first time my daddy ever give me advice that I thought wasn't worth the two pennies he claimed for it.

I was so sure he would understand. I thought his big, soft heart that couldn't stand to kill a Nazi wouldn't have nothing against an innocent colored girl.

I knew then that Imogene was right all along. Her being colored and me being white meant there was a muddy wide river between her people and mine. And it was going to take a powerful strong bridge to get our people across it.

23

The Wheelchair
November 1944–January 1945

The next couple of months was like another wide river to cross. In some ways, time dragged like the end of a long school year. But in other ways, a lot happened to keep me occupied.

In November, President Roosevelt got reelected to his fourth term. I knew he would, even though I seen in the newspapers that plenty of people was against him. Some people said Roosevelt was going to die before he made it through his fourth term. His health was failing. His picture in the papers showed dark circles under his eyes, but I thought he could stand up to anything after licking polio the way he did.

After the election, I worked up my nerve to ask Dr. Bennett about him. He was the main doctor at Roosevelt's polio center in Warm Springs, Georgia. And he come to our hospital every so often. He usually watched the physiotherapists check our muscles to see how much progress we made.

"Do you actually get close to the president?" I asked Dr. Bennett. "Does he talk to you?"

Dr. Bennett laughed softly. When he did that, his high forehead wrinkled and his kind eyes squinted almost shut. "The president talks to everybody," he said. "If the Secret

Service will let him, that is. And there's a chance I'll see him in a few weeks. He likes to be in Warm Springs at Thanksgiving to eat turkey with his polio friends."

"You mean he actually eats with the patients?" I asked. I was so interested in the conversation I didn't notice if Miss Ruth's exercises was paining me or not.

"Yes indeed. And they entertain him with talent shows and special programs. Why, young lady, you could be down there performing for the president one day."

You could've knocked me out of bed with my daddy's big red handkerchief when he said that. "Wh-what do you mean?" I asked.

"Other patients from this hospital have gone there," said Dr. Bennett. "Right now, there's more we can do for you here. So keep working. But later, when you've reached a certain point in your recovery, you could be just the kind of person who'd go to Warm Springs. You'd get excellent care and more therapy."

I tell you what's the truth—it felt like my breath got snatched nearly right out of my chest when he said that. "But, sir," I said, "I could never afford to go to Warm Springs."

Dr. Bennett shook his head. "Warm Springs isn't for the wealthy," he said. "We have some beds for people who can't pay. Or a businessman from your community might want to sponsor you."

When he said that, I thought about Peggy Sue's daddy, who owns that hosiery mill. But I didn't tell Dr. Bennett about him. I was still trying to get used to the idea of me going to Warm Springs.

"Are you pulling my leg?" I asked.

Dr. Bennett busted out laughing when I said that. "No," he said. "Miss Ruth's the one pulling your leg. But I'm serious

BLUE

about you and Warm Springs." He reached over and gave my foot a little tug. Then he moved on to the next patient—like it was any old conversation we just had.

That Dr. Bennett didn't have no idea how weak and woozy I felt all of a sudden.

In December, the people of Hickory put on special programs for us. That was fun, but the best thing about Christmas was that I got a wheelchair. It belonged to the hospital, of course. But Miss Ruth acted like Santa brought it just for me.

My heart was pounding like a drum when they brought me that big wooden chair. It had a fancy cane back and wooden footrests and wheels on each side that had spokes like a bicycle.

At first I could hardly make the chair move because my muscles was so weak. But Miss Ruth worked with me. "Talk to those muscles," she said. When I finally got it to move a few inches, all the other girls hollered and clapped and acted like a baby had just took its first steps.

Somehow I made it to the end of the ward. Which wasn't easy because the chair was big and I kept bumping into beds.

After that, I got out of bed every chance I could. The girls who was stuck in beds begged me to visit them in my wheelchair. I'd read the funny papers to them and tell them what I was reading in the newspapers.

Every time we seen Roosevelt's picture in the paper or a magazine, we put it on a bulletin board at the end of the ward. One of the girls who was real artistic cut out black and yellow letters that said OUR HERO. At the bottom of the board she wrote his famous saying: *The only thing we have to fear is fear itself.*

Having the president right there on our bulletin board was like having our own guardian angel. It was like he was looking over the room and saying, *If I can do it, you can too.*

I liked to lay in my bed and look at him there. I could almost hear him saying something more—just to me. To me he was saying, *Ann Fay Honeycutt, I'll be seeing you in Warm Springs, Georgia.*

Roosevelt's birthday was on January 30. It was a big day for polio patients. It seemed like every town in America held a President's Birthday Ball, and the money they raised from them dances went to the March of Dimes to pay for things like my wheelchair.

January was the month for the March of Dimes to raise money for polio. They printed a booklet called "The Miracle of Hickory" so everyone in America could see how much good they done when they give their dimes for polio. That booklet told how our hospital went up in no time flat, and how everyone in the community pitched in.

Well, I knew it was a miracle hospital, but still, I was getting plumb bored in that place. One day I got so bored that I started dreaming up ways to keep from going crazy. It suddenly crossed my mind that my chair could take me to see Imogene.

Then I got to thinking how Imogene was in a wheelchair too. She had got hers even before me. Maybe we could meet halfway.

I didn't know if those nurses read the letters they took back and forth for us. So I thought we might have to come up with some kind of code. And then I realized we already had a code—from Momma and Imogene talking about bridges and muddy rivers. So I wrote:

Dear Imogene,

How are you? I'm bored. I miss you like always. I was thinking about that bridge my mother mentioned to me once and that muddy wide river you was talking about. I was thinking maybe we could meet halfway. Why wait for someone else to build a bridge when you and me both have what it takes already?

The way I see it, if Roosevelt could get in the White House, the rest of us can get out of this place if we put our minds to it.

I go all over the ward in my wheelchair. But this ward is too small and I'm about to go plumb out of my mind. Sometimes I just want to bust out of here.

What are you doing on Saturday night around 11:00? I sure wish I could see you again.

Your friend always,

Ann Fay Honeycutt

I picked Saturday because not so many people worked weekends now that the epidemic was over. At night, the nurses would sit at their work station and write letters to the soldiers overseas, doing their part for the war. And some of them would nod off every now and again.

Well, when I got Imogene's letter, I could see right away she caught my meaning.

Dear Ann Fay,

I'm working on getting out of here. I just keep talking to my muscles. And every now and then they take a notion to do what I say.

Ain't no river so wide we can't cross it. It took me a minute to figure out your meaning. But I know we'll both

BLUE

cross at the proper time. Be careful and don't forget to say
your prayers.
    Your friend,
        Imogene Wilfong

It was Thursday when we swapped those letters. When Saturday night come, it started raining before most of the girls had went to sleep. I groaned and pulled my pillow over my head. I could tell from the way it was driving against my window that it wouldn't let up for a while.

Then I got to thinking that the rain might help us. Nobody would expect two patients to go outside in this weather.

By this time I could get into my wheelchair by myself. The nurses had got to where they left it by my bed. So that was a help too.

Nurse Amanda nodded off and took to snoring about 10:45. I pulled my chenille housecoat on overtop of my hospital gown.

When the clock on the wall said 11:00, the girls was mostly sleeping. But I could tell that Betsy, whose bed was right by the door, was still awake. I could hear her humming to herself. I was afraid she'd give me away if she seen me go out the door.

But first I had to get past Nurse Amanda. She was sleeping with her head on the side of a bed. She fell asleep singing "I Couldn't Sleep a Wink Last Night" to Shelby, one of the little girls.

A floorboard creaked right when I went past her. Nurse Amanda stopped snoring. She opened her eyes and looked at me and then she pulled her head up fast. "Where are you going, Ann Fay?"

Well, I couldn't just tell her I was going outside in the rain to see Imogene.

Then Nurse Amanda answered her own question. "To the bathroom?" she asked. "Need any help?"

I started breathing again. "No, I can handle it," I said. Nurse Amanda kept her eye on me, which I reckon was her job. So I went to the bathroom even though I was losing precious time. I sure hoped Imogene wasn't going to give up on me.

I stayed in the bathroom with the door open a crack till I heard Nurse Amanda snoring again. Then I come out as quiet as I could. I wheeled fast to the door at the end of the ward. I opened it and started to push my wheelchair through.

Betsy said, "Hey, Ann Fay, where you going?"

I jerked my head around to see if Nurse Amanda heard, and I seen then that she opened her eyes for a second. But I don't think they was open long enough to focus on anything because she went right back to sleep.

"Shhh!" I said to Betsy. "Don't wake the nurse. It's a surprise." And just like that, I went out the door.

I didn't have no experience riding that wheelchair over the wet boards on the ramp outside. At first I thought I might jolt myself right out of the chair. But once that chair started rolling down that ramp, it just kept going. Just when I thought I was going to go flying, it landed with a jolt and a crunch on the dirt at the end of the ramp.

Suddenly those wheels didn't want to go nowhere. I grabbed them with my hands and pushed with all my might. But my muscles was weak, especially the ones in my left arm.

The rain was coming down hard now, and I knew I couldn't just sit there and get soaking wet for no reason at all. So I started talking to those muscles. "Get your lazy bones moving," I told them.

I put my whole mind to moving those wheels just the

tiniest bit, and I felt them turn. I yelled at my muscles some more. "Get a move on it. Giddy up!" The wheels moved some more, and I could see I was getting off the soft muddy area and onto the solid ground of the hospital driveway. I closed my eyes and pushed on those wheels with everything I had in me. I imagined a river and me trying to swim across it.

And next thing I knew, I was moving along and the chair was rolling almost easy. I headed toward the building Imogene was in. At first I didn't see no sign of her. But then I heard her laugh and seen her dark shape come around the side of the building.

She done it! Somehow she had got out. We headed toward each other, our wheelchairs moving like two boats on a dark river. We was practically swimming with all that rain coming down on us.

When we got close we reached out and grabbed ahold of each other's arms and laughed. Imogene threw back her head and laughed a big belly laugh and I did too. We opened our mouths and let the rain fall inside.

In the light coming out of the building beside us, I seen the rain collecting in little drops on Imogene's hair. It seemed like her hair wasn't even getting wet and mine was all soaked. The water was running off me like a river. Imogene laughed. "I could wring you out like a dishrag," she said.

By then my teeth was chattering. "I c-could use you to m-mop the floor," I said.

"The dishrag and the mop," said Imogene. "That us." She laughed again. "And I got a feeling, somebody is gonna mop the floor with us when they finds us here."

"Well," I said, "they won't need no bucket of water, will they?" I lifted my hands and Imogene's too. We danced a

BLUE

little hand dance back and forth in the air and threw back our heads and squealed. I felt the rain run down my face and drip off my chin.

Then I heard Nurse Amanda hollering, and I knew she had caught us already.

24

The "Miracle of Hickory"

January–February 1945

Nurse Amanda stuck me and Imogene in one of them clover-shaped metal tubs they put us in for therapy. I was chilled to the core, and the warm water felt twice as good as it ever done when I was in it for exercises.

"If you catch your death of cold, don't blame it on anyone but yourselves," Nurse Amanda grumbled. "And see if I don't start watching you girls like a hawk over a chicken yard."

She always acted like she didn't understand why me and Imogene wanted to be friends, but I had a feeling that she was secretly proud of us.

"If you can put your mind to riding wheelchairs around in the rain," she said, "then I know you can learn to walk again. I expect you to be out of this place before they close it down and move you off to Charlotte."

"What!" I cried. "Who's moving to Charlotte?"

Amanda forced her lips into a pretend hard line and said, "I thought you read the newspapers, Ann Fay. They're talking about closing this hospital down."

"I been reading those articles for months," I said. "And they ain't shut it down yet. It's just rumors."

"Don't be so sure. The epidemic is officially over and most patients have gone home. I suppose the politicians want to save money. So they're talking about taking the rest of you to Charlotte Memorial. You girls had better shape up because they won't put up with your nonsense over there."

"Charlotte is too far away," I said. "My mother won't be able to come visit. Why can't they send us to Hickory Memorial?"

"Hickory Memorial doesn't have a polio ward. Charlotte is better equipped to take polio patients."

"I'm not going," I said. "I'm fixing to get out of here."

"Me too," said Imogene. "I'm not going to another hospital for true."

I laughed just thinking how much we sounded like Ida and Ellie—me whining like Ida, and Imogene whining the same little whine I whined first.

Sometimes I did feel like the two of us was almost twin sisters.

Nurse Amanda said, "Well then, I'll tell your physios to work you extra hard so you can get out of here before they move you to the big city."

And I reckon she did, because when Miss Ruth come for my therapy session on Monday, she had a wicked gleam in her eye. "So," she said, "I hear you're getting out soon. That means we've got work to do." She began working the muscles in my legs and telling me to talk to them.

I was tired of talking to my muscles. But I could see that it worked, so I did it anyway. For weeks I fussed at them. I told them what Daddy always told me. "The first step is the hardest!" I told them Daddy was coming home from the war and I had to be out of the hospital when he did. Which I didn't know if it was true, but I didn't mind lying to my muscles. I told them I wasn't about to go to that Charlotte hospital.

And I told them the sooner they started working right,

the sooner they could go to Warm Springs—and see the president. I still didn't hardly believe it myself, so just in case my muscles wasn't convinced, I told them Dr. Bennett said so.

I begged the doctors to order me a pair of braces. Especially Dr. Hahn, who was in charge of the hospital. When it come to polio patients, his heart was big as the town of Hickory. I reckon he seen how hard I was working, because before long I had me that pair of braces.

By February I had some movement in my right leg. Miss Ruth had tears in her eyes when she seen me move it. Me and her had got real attached to each other.

"Keep working," she said. "And don't be in such a hurry to go home. You need the help of a therapist to get as much movement back as you can." I knew it was her way of telling me I'd probably have to go to Charlotte whether I liked it or not.

But she said if they moved us to Charlotte, she wouldn't be going along. "I'm going into the service," she said. "It's time for me to help the war effort."

By the middle of February, talk about shutting down the emergency hospital was serious. The patients didn't want to go. The nurses and physios was sad too. If the hospital shut down, some of them was heading back to where they come from—Florida, California, Massachusetts, and who knows where else.

After all we been through together, we felt like we was one big family. And now we might have to break up.

Sure enough—Nurse Amanda was right. Next thing I knew, the papers announced that the patients at the Hickory Polio Center was definitely moving to Charlotte.

The newspaper had lots of articles about our hospital.

Everybody was bragging on what a good job the nurses done. And there was an article about someone who was in New York City and seen a movie about our hospital. He said they showed the Miracle of Hickory movie right out on the street where thousands of people could see it when they walked by.

I knew some movie people from Hollywood had come and took pictures of the hospital. And they even brought it back to Hickory so we could see it. But I couldn't imagine a movie screen right out on the street.

What I couldn't figure out was—if our hospital was so wonderful and famous, why did they want to shut it down?

25

Charlotte Memorial
March–April 1945

When they moved us to Charlotte, there was more digni-
taries making speeches and getting their pictures taken than
you could shake a stick at. And Momma was there too. She
helped me pack up my belongings. We hung on to each
other and I promised I would work hard and get out of that
Charlotte hospital quick as I could.

I was one of the first people out of the building. They
moved the ones in wheelchairs first. I begged Nurse Amanda
to put me in a car with Imogene.

"Young lady," she said, "what you're asking for—it just
isn't natural."

The hospital grounds was covered with police, firemen,
and all sorts of bigwigs. Not to mention a line of black cars
stretched out past the main highway. I kept trying to see
Imogene through the crowd, but there was too much commotion. And I figured the coloreds would be the last ones
out.

When it was time to go, Momma give me one last squeeze
and Nurse Amanda pushed my chair to the door of a shiny
black car. She told the volunteers to put me in the back seat.
"No," I said. "I'm waiting on Imogene. Where is she?"

But Amanda just shook her head and grumbled something about white people sticking with their own kind. And

the next thing I knew, a fireman was lifting me into the car.

I about jumped out of my skin when I heard a voice beside me. "It's about time you gets yourself in this car."

"Imogene!" I screamed. "You're done already here!" I grabbed her hand, and we laughed so hard I forgot to say thank you to the fireman. Then my door got shut and it was just the two of us there in the back seat. "How did you get here?" I asked. And then I seen a white face up behind Imogene's black one. It was Nurse Amanda peeking in the car window. I thought her cheeks was going to split wide open from that smile on her face. But I seen tears in her eyes too.

"Nurse Amanda say this her goodbye present to me and you," Imogene explained.

Nurse Amanda waved and disappeared. She had more patients to load into cars.

The driver was a gentleman who introduced himself as Mr. Barger. His wife must've been out talking to some friends. She got into the car just when it was time for him to move forward so another car could load up. Mrs. Barger's mouth fell open when she seen Imogene in her car. Her husband said, "It's all right, dear. She's here by special arrangement."

"Oh," said the woman, and that was the end of that.

At first we moved real slow out of the hospital grounds. When I seen all the nurses and Miss Ruth waving out the hospital windows, the tears started running. I felt like I was leaving my home and family. And Momma was gonna be so far away and probably couldn't visit again.

They said the line of cars taking us to Charlotte was a mile long. Every little town we went through, the cars all blew their horns. Ambulances and police cars turned on their sirens so the people of the towns would see us coming.

Me and Imogene held hands and talked about the Charlotte hospital. "Probably it's fancy," I said. "But I'd rather be back in that tent they had us in at first."

"A tent is fine by me if you in it," said Imogene.

"You know they're gonna split us like a piece of firewood," I said.

And I was right, too. When we got to Charlotte, some orderlies brought wheelchairs. One orderly stopped dead in his tracks when he seen Imogene.

"Whoa!" he said. "Something's not right." He looked at Imogene. "Missy, you're in the wrong place for sure."

Him and the driver had a conversation about how they was going to get her to the colored ward. Finally the driver said he would push her there in one of the wheelchairs and his wife could drive the car when the line got to moving again.

I give Imogene a big hug.

"Write to me, dishrag," said Imogene.

"Yes, mophead," I said. "But who's going to deliver our letters?"

"We'll find someone," said Imogene.

Then the orderly was helping me out of the car, and the driver was helping Imogene into her chair on the other side. The last I seen of her was through the two back doors of that car. I had a feeling like I would never see Imogene Wilfong again.

The Charlotte hospital was good and bad. The good part was they had lots of fun things to do. A circus come to perform just for us polio patients. And Danny Moury's daddy come and showed us some moving pictures he took with his little movie camera of the "Miracle of Hickory" hospital. It didn't have a real movie star talking on it like the one the Hollywood people made. In fact, it didn't have no talking at all. But I liked it on account of I had got to know Danny's momma and daddy on visiting days. Danny was a little boy who come to the emergency hospital about the same time I did.

The hospital wasn't fancy like I expected. Well, I reckon parts of it might have been. But not the polio ward. It was built for the epidemic, like the Hickory hospital, but it wasn't as good as ours by a long shot.

There was only one bathroom for the whole ward full of us girls. Which meant it was busy all the time. The nurses would take the bedpans from the girls and line them up outside the bathroom door, waiting for the orderlies to come and empty them and spray them out. So it smelled pretty awful sometimes, especially on hot days. And it was starting to get hot already.

But the worst part about being in Charlotte was how lonely I felt. Momma wrote Daddy about me moving, so after a while I started getting some letters from him at the Charlotte hospital. I had wrote to him about maybe going to Warm Springs. At first I thought he might not believe me. But he wrote me right back and I knew that just like he always said, Daddy believed I could do whatever I put my mind to.

Dear Ann Fay,

If anybody deserves to see the president it's you for sure. If he knew all you have done to take care of your family he would give you a medal. Keep working hard and you will make it to Warm Springs. It does my heart good to hear about the progress you're making.

We are making progress here too. I hope and pray it won't be much longer.

All my love,

Daddy

My daddy saying it, helped me to believe it. But first, I just wanted to go home for a while.

It was spring now and I was thinking how a year ago I was planting my daddy's garden. I felt bad because my momma was taking care of the girls and making the garden too. I wanted to help her. I missed the smell of the crumbly red dirt and the feel of it damp between my toes.

One night I dreamed I was in the garden. Just when I yanked the pull start on the tiller, Junior Bledsoe come and took the tiller away from me. He pointed to my legs, and I seen that they was all shriveled up to two thin sticks that wouldn't even bend.

"Ann Fay Honeycutt," he said. "You couldn't run a tiller when you had two good legs. How do you expect to do it with them sticks?" He made me so mad I started kicking my legs and throwing a temper tantrum.

And then I woke up and I really was kicking my legs and I could feel that my left knee—my weak one—had even moved a little.

That's when I knew I would be walking soon.

When they brought my breakfast, I said I didn't want to eat. I just wanted to see my physio. But of course I had to wait till it suited her.

While I was waiting, I got in my wheelchair and went to the bathroom. I held my breath going past all them bedpans lined up in the hall.

I was just about finished doing my business when the door opened and a colored orderly walked in with a bedpan. I was so shocked I just about fell in that toilet. And I was so embarrassed I wished he would just flush me right down.

But I think he was more embarrassed than me, even. He backed out of there with his eyes closed and said, "Excuse me, miss. Excuse me for true. I didn't know you was in here."

When he shut that door, I prayed he wouldn't never have to come back on my ward again, because I didn't think I could look him in the eye. But I knew he would. He was there every day whistling one of them Negro songs Imogene sometimes like to sing.

I finished up and got back in my chair and opened the door. I kept my eyes on the floor all the way back to the ward, but I had a feeling he was hiding from me too, because I didn't see no man's shoes along the way. And I for sure didn't hear no whistling.

I sat in the wheelchair by my bed and waited for my physio.

In Charlotte, my physio was Miss Jane. She had the same pretty brown eyes as Miss Ruth, but they didn't have the same sparkle and she wasn't as talkative as Miss Ruth. Still, I thought she would be excited to see me bending my knee.

She seen I was determined and started working real hard with me. I didn't tell her I was going to Warm Springs for more therapy, and I for sure didn't mention seeing the president—she'd think I was imagining things. Sometimes I thought so myself, but I never stopped thinking about it. I started improving fast. My left knee was still stiff, but I knew I could make it bend more if I just kept talking to it.

I asked Miss Jane did she know a patient named Imogene Wilfong who come from Hickory.

"No," she said. "We don't have any patients by that name."

"She's in the colored ward."

Miss Jane didn't say nothing at first. Then she said, "I don't work in the colored ward. The coloreds are in tents outside the hospital."

That made me mad. "Tents?" I said. "Tents is what they

had in Hickory at the worst part of the epidemic. Tents is supposed to be for temporary. And y'all went and put the coloreds in a tent? How do they stay warm on cold nights?"

"Well, these tents are for temporary," said Miss Jane. "We're in the same epidemic Hickory had. And the weather is getting warmer, so don't worry your pretty head over a few coloreds."

"If Charlotte couldn't do no better by coloreds than putting them in a tent, then why did they shut down our Hickory hospital? That place was a pure miracle."

Miss Jane tugged on my leg and said, "I know all about your 'Miracle of Hickory.' It's been in all the magazines. And the movies even. But I didn't shut it down."

"Well," I said, "I know it ain't your fault, but could you do me a big favor?"

Miss Jane didn't make me no promises. She just waited for me to ask.

"Imogene Wilfong is my friend," I said. "I wrote her a letter. Would you take it to her for me? And get one from her too, on account of I know she wrote me."

Miss Jane started shaking her head before I even finished. "I never go to the colored ward," she said. "They got their own help over there."

I begged and pleaded and promised to work hard and get out of there real fast if she did. But all my begging didn't do me one bit of good. Miss Jane just shook her head.

I knew I was going to have to find another way to get to Imogene.

26

The President
April 1945

My letters to Imogene piled up on the table beside my bed and slid off on the floor. I asked nurses and even the doctors to deliver them. But it seemed like everybody was just too busy. Or else they didn't care.

I thought maybe if none of them white people was going to help me, at least a colored person might. But the only colored person I ever seen was that one orderly named Harvey who walked in on me while I was in the bathroom. And I tried not to see him. Every time I heard his whistling coming my direction, I turned my face away.

I kept thinking if I was going to get my letters to Imogene I was going to have to ask him. But I kept hoping to find someone else.

Then one day something happened that changed everything. It was April 12, 1945, and I will never forget it as long as I live. It was late in the day when I heard a big commotion at the nurses' station. I was stuck in my bed, but I could tell something important had happened in the world. The nurse at the other end of the ward went rushing out of the room, saying, "Oh, dear God in heaven. What will America do now?"

All the staff was out in the nurses' area, listening to a radio which they had turned up so loud I could almost make out what it was saying. Almost, but not quite. I seen through the door to where them nurses was crying on each other's shoulders. Whatever the news was, I knew it wasn't good.

My heart sagged. It must be something about the war. Was it another bombing like at Pearl Harbor? Just when we thought it would soon be over?

The girls in the ward started to holler out. "What happened? Tell us."

I was sliding out of my bed, fixing to get into that wheelchair, when Harvey stepped into the room. His lips was trembling, but he put his finger over them and we all got quiet. I seen his Adam's apple sliding up and down in his neck and I knew something had really upset him.

Finally Harvey spoke. "It's our president," he said. "Mr. Franklin Delano Roosevelt died this afternoon at his polio place in Warm Springs, Georgia."

And then Harvey's face twisted, and he walked away quick before we seen him cry.

The whole ward got so quiet we really could hear the radio in the hall. Only thing was—now we wanted it shut off. Now I wanted to rush out in my wheelchair and smash that radio.

How could it be? What would we do without our president? All of America looked to Roosevelt to lead us out of this war.

A deep sadness settled over the hospital. Church bells rung all over town, and it felt to me like the whole town was crying.

People said it was a shame the president didn't live to hear them bells announce the end of the war. They said it could be over any day now.

The aides tiptoed around our beds, and Harvey didn't

BLUE

whistle his cheerful hymns like always. Instead he hummed a song Imogene used to sing sometimes when we was getting those Kenny packs.

Nobody knows the trouble I see,
Nobody knows my sorrow;
Nobody knows the trouble I see,
Glory hallelujah!

I hadn't felt this alone since my daddy left. I needed Imogene in the bed beside me. I needed her people's wisdom to comfort me.

But Imogene was in the colored tent.

I didn't eat none of my supper that night. I just kept thinking how I come so close to seeing the president. So close to going to Warm Springs and eating Thanksgiving dinner with him or being in one of them talent shows.

I should've known it was too good to be true. It was too much to believe that a poor country girl like me could get anywheres close to the president of the United States—especially one as great as Franklin Delano Roosevelt.

The next day, the radio announced that Roosevelt's body was coming north on a train. Some of the nurses said they was going out to the train station that night. I asked one of them could she please take me with her. But I knew it wasn't possible.

It just didn't seem right that none of us with polio could pay our respects. I knew Roosevelt would not be happy about that. He would want us lined up by the train tracks in our wheelchairs and iron lungs.

But nobody asked me what I knew about it.

It was pure quiet in the ward that night. Nobody moved

BLUE

around unless they had to, and then it was like they felt it was a desecration if their heels clicked on the floor or they bumped into something by accident.

I think we was all listening for the sound of that train going through Charlotte.

The next morning one of the nurses walked into our ward with a bouquet of flowers and started handing one to every patient. "This flower was bought by the Lions Club to honor the president," she said to each one. "It was in the train station when he went through last night. They sent it just for you."

That's when I knew that someone really did understand about us. I sucked in the sweet smell of that yellow rosebud, and it spread a sadness and a joy over me all at the same time. I thought how I would keep that rose till the day I died.

I'd show it to Peggy Sue and Junior Bledsoe and Reverend Price. I'd say, "Don't feel sorry for me on account of I had polio. Look here what I got. I got one of the president's roses. That's one thing polio done for me."

When a hospital volunteer finally brought me a newspaper, I read all about the president's body coming through Charlotte. The paper said the president would have liked them giving the flowers to us polios. It said Roosevelt would have called that grand.

I read how thousands of people come out to meet him. And how a group of singers sung "Onward, Christian Soldiers." And everyone stood in silence and cried when the casket went by real slow.

The paper said Negroes were down at the other end of the station, singing spirituals. It said they looked upon Roosevelt as the best friend they ever had in the White House.

And that's when it hit me. That's when I got to wondering—did anyone take the president's flowers to the colored tent?

I thought I knew the answer to that question. And then I knew what I had to do.

I wanted that yellow rose. I wanted to take it home and put it in the little cedar box my daddy made me last Christmas. Whenever I needed extra courage, I would take it out and think about the man with polio who become the president.

But I kept thinking how Imogene didn't have one of the president's flowers. And if anyone deserved to have one, it was Imogene Wilfong for sure.

But didn't I deserve it too? After putting up with them hot packs, and exercising my muscles for months, and missing my family the whole time?

And then I thought how Imogene went through everything I did. It was Imogene that got me through them hot packs in the first place. And wasn't it Imogene who told me that God keeps my tears in a blue bottle all my own?

I knew that with Roosevelt dying, Imogene was over there in the colored tent making tears for that brown-and-rainbow-colored bottle that God was keeping on her. Imogene had brought comfort to me when I needed it. Now it was my turn to comfort her.

I felt empty just thinking about my little cedar box without that yellow rose. But my head was full of voices. I heard President Roosevelt saying in his great radio voice, *The only thing we have to fear is fear itself.* I heard Daddy saying, *If Roosevelt can be president and he can't even walk, you can handle anything that—* Then Imogene's voice butted in: *It mostly hurts at first. After a while it starts to feel better.*

Well, right that minute it was sure hurting. And I didn't

have no one to give me the courage to do what I had to do. Not my daddy or my momma and not even Imogene. All I had was a yellow rose.

I figured every man and woman in the country would give their right arm to have one of the president's roses. They'd be proud to put that yellow rose in a little box on their mantelpiece. Then when company come around, they'd open the box and say, "Look at what I got—a rose from when the president's funeral train went through Charlotte." And their friends would say, all hushed and reverent, "How about that! That's something you don't see every day."

If I give that rose up now, nobody would believe I ever had it.

But if I kept it, it would always remind me how I didn't have the courage to do what I needed to when I had the chance.

Well, I knew I couldn't count on the nurses to run it all the way out to the colored tent. There was only one person who might do it.

The next time I heard Harvey whistling, I fixed my eyes on that yellow rose and called his name real quick before I could change my mind.

Harvey looked up from the floor he was mopping in our ward. "Yes, miss?"

"I was wondering, could you do me a favor?"

Harvey stood quiet and said, "Yes, miss, I'm sure I would be glad to."

I pointed to the rose that was in a cup of water. "I need you to take this rose to someone."

Harvey whistled softly. "Is that the president's rose you giving away?"

"I want you to take it to Imogene Wilfong," I said. "She's in the tent for colored polios."

Harvey shook his head like he was trying to figure out if he heard me right. Like he was shaking some confusion out. "You giving the president's rose to a colored girl?"

"I don't figure they give any of the president's roses to the colored patients."

"No, miss," said Harvey. "I don't reckons they did."

When Harvey reached for the rose on the table he seen my stack of letters to Imogene. "You want I should take these too?" he asked.

"The letters! Of course. I almost forgot."

"Well, I think I'm gonna need me a sack," said Harvey. And then he took off looking for one. When he come back, he put all the letters in a brown paper bag. "I'll come back for everything later," he said. "When I gets off work, I'll come and get it."

I wrote one more letter to Imogene.

Dear Imogene,

I reckon you heard the sad news. I reckon everyone has heard. They give us each a rose that was bought just to honor the president when his train come through town. I want you to have mine. Yellow roses always dry real nice, so I know it will keep for a long time. Keep it forever and always think of me and the best president this country ever had.

Your friend,

Ann Fay Honeycutt

I hoped if Imogene seen the teardrops on the letter, she would think it was because of the president and not worry about me being sad to give up my rose.

When Harvey come for the rose, I sucked in its smell one last time—long and hard—till it filled me with courage.

Harvey stood there so quiet and respectful with his hand on his heart, like I was holding the president's funeral or something. Which I reckon I was, if you want to know the truth.

I told Harvey how to find Imogene. "She's the pretty one with the green eyes," I said.

Harvey just grinned and walked away with my bag of letters and the president's yellow rose. He was singing, *"There's a yellow rose in Texas that I am going to see ..."*

It seemed like that Harvey had a song for everything that happened in this world.

27

Victory!

May–June 1945

At first when our president died, I wondered if we could win this war without him. But I reckon he still led us through. Things ended quick, just like people was saying they would. The last day of April, Hitler killed himself—which was a sure sign the war wasn't going his way. Then about a week later the Germans surrendered.

Church bells rung all over town, and for a minute you didn't know whether to be sad because of Roosevelt not getting to hear them or happy because it meant the war was over. But the happiness took over, and then you should've heard the noise in the polio ward. Such a whooping and a hollering! We all started talking how our daddies and brothers would be coming home.

Harvey stopped whistling and humming and went to outright singing.

I ain't gwine study war no more,
Ain't gwine study war no more,
Ain't gwine study war no more ...

I started thinking my daddy was coming home. But then people said our boys wasn't coming home right away. They still had work to do in Europe, cleaning up after the war and helping lost people find homes again. And some of them would be shipped to islands in the Pacific Ocean to fight the Japanese, who was doing their best to take what part of the world Hitler hadn't got his hands on.

The war wasn't really over yet. Not until the Japanese surrendered too.

I prayed my daddy wouldn't have to go to the Pacific. If he couldn't come home, I prayed he would get to help rebuild Europe. As much as he hated the killing, maybe now he could do something he felt good about. I give up on the idea of seeing him soon, and I tried hard not to be selfish about it.

I put all my attention to seeing Momma and the girls. My physio said I could go home soon. My left leg was still weak, but I promised to do my exercises every day. And with a special brace and crutches, I was learning to walk. It wore me plumb out, but I practiced every day. I was determined to get out of that hospital.

I decided that after I was home awhile I would probably still go to Warm Springs. Dr. Bennett come to Charlotte to check on us every so often, and he was still making plans for me to go.

It wouldn't be the same as going while Roosevelt was alive. But I had a feeling that just being in Warm Springs, breathing the air he breathed—just that would give me the courage to face anything that come my way.

Imogene went home before the war was even over. It seemed like just when we got Harvey to deliver our letters, she left me. I was happy for her. Of course I was. But me, I was lonelier than ever. Well, at least I had her address. And I was going to write for sure. And she had already sent me one letter.

Dear Ann Fay,

See why I picked you out a blue color for your bottle? Because of you being true as the sky above. When that Harvey told me that yellow rose was the president's flower, I told him to take it right on back to you. But he said that would be a slap in your face, and I knew he was right.

Well, I tell you what—I cried when I heard our president was dead, and I cried even more when I got that rose. I reckons that brown-and-rainbow-colored bottle on God's windowsill is full and running over.

I'm home now and my momma is trying to fatten me with biscuits and fried chicken and all other kinds of home cooking.

I put that rose in my momma's china cabinet with the glass door. No one can touch it. But everybody who sets foot in this house has to look at it if I have anything to say about it.

I won't ever forget the one who gave it to me.
Your friend,
Imogene Wilfong

When I read Imogene's letter, I decided that the minute I got home I would put it in my little cedar box in the place of the president's yellow rose.

Finally, right before the Fourth of July, the hospital sent a letter to Momma telling her to pick me up on the weekend. I knew Junior would have to bring her. I was anxious to see him again too. And his mother and Peggy Sue and the Hinkle sisters and Reverend Price and just everybody.

That Saturday morning was sunny and hot. I was awake before daylight and I couldn't get back to sleep. I thought I would jump plumb out of my skin, waiting on Momma and

Junior to get there. My bag of letters and personal items was packed and ready. But I was still wearing a hospital gown because I had to wait on Momma to bring me some clothes.

It made me sad to think how they took my overalls off and probably burnt them when I went to the Hickory hospital. Them overalls was a sign of strength to me. They made me want to do for my family so Daddy would be proud. I could hear his voice plain as yesterday, saying, "I expect you to be the man of the house while I'm gone."

My daddy's voice never left me. It was what got me through all that work in the garden, taking care of my sisters while Momma and Bobby was at the hospital, and struggling to walk again.

I stood at the window, straining to see my daddy's truck outside. I kept looking for Momma and Junior to come across that parking lot, but I didn't see them.

Then I heard a voice behind me. "Ann Fay Honeycutt, are you coming home with me or not?" And it was his voice. It was my daddy's voice. It scared me so bad to hear it like that, so unexpected. I was afraid to look because I knew I must've heard it in my head.

But I turned and there he stood—and not in his uniform neither. He was wearing black Sunday pants and his long-sleeved blue shirt with the sleeves rolled half up. His eyes was the color of overalls. And truth. And faithfulness.

And wisteria blossoms.

I couldn't run to him but I forgot that I couldn't, so I tried to. And I went crashing to the floor. Then my daddy run to me. He sunk to his knees and pulled me to him. "Daddy," I said. "Why are you here? I didn't know. Oh, Daddy, I didn't expect you." We sat on the floor and both of us cried till his shirt pocket was all wet.

Momma was there too. Daddy stood and helped me to my feet and pulled both of us into his big arms. I felt that broken-up feeling again because the girls and Bobby wasn't there. But I knew I would feel it for the rest of my life, so I'd just have to get used to it.

Momma handed me a bag and told me to go get dressed. When I reached inside, I found my blue overalls—the ones Daddy give me when he went away. I just couldn't believe it. "But I thought they burned them," I said.

"No," said Momma. "They boiled them along with the rest of the laundry at the hospital. And when I came to visit, they returned them to me."

"But you never told me."

Momma just smiled and give me a quick kiss on the forehead. "I must've forgot," she said.

Daddy's truck was parked at the entrance to the polio ward. And Ida and Ellie was hanging out the window when we got there. They would've knocked me over if Momma hadn't held them back. "Girls," she said, "your sister's on crutches. You're just going to have to get it in your heads, she isn't as strong as she used to be."

I didn't like Momma saying that, and Daddy knew I didn't. When we was all squeezed into that truck, he said, "Well, if you ask me, Ann Fay is tougher than ever."

He turned the key and pressed the starter button and said, "Who's going to help me shift this thing?"

I knew he meant me because I was straddling the gear stick, which come up out of the floor. But after a minute I noticed another reason he wanted me to shift. He wasn't using his right arm to drive. Just his left one.

"What happened to your arm, Daddy?" I asked.

He shrugged. "Nothing much, honey. Just a little war

wound in the shoulder. It's the reason they sent me home early. But I'll be all right. As long as I got your right arm, I can do without mine."

We drove home like that, Daddy steering and pushing the pedals and me shifting the gears. I knew I was as put together as I could get. The best part of me was home again. He had a good left leg and I had a good right arm and that was enough for me.

Daddy said he would take us to a diner to celebrate, but I said I was dying to get home. I said I'd help cook the dinner if they'd just take me there.

Ida started into whining right off. "But Daddy, you promised."

And Ellie said, "Yeah, Daddy."

Daddy said, "Ann Fay gets to decide. It's her big day."

"Well, then," I said. "Let's stop off for a root beer." So we did. But the whole time we was sitting on the bench outside that gas station, each of us drinking our very own dope, I just wanted to get back in that truck and drive out into the country.

Just before I emptied my bottle, Daddy said, "Ann Fay, I brought you something back from the war." Then he walked over to the pickup and reached under the seat for something he had put there. It was a brown paper sack. He brought it back and said, "Go ahead. Look inside."

All I wanted Daddy to bring me from the war was himself. I couldn't imagine what else he had. I looked inside and there was a bunch of papers all folded up together. I thought maybe they was wrapped around something fragile, so I pulled them out real careful and unfolded them, and I just couldn't believe what I seen.

Them pages was covered with pictures of tigers and lions

and elephants, and on the bottom of every one it said, *Good night, sleep tight, don't let the bedbugs bite.*

Well, I reckon my daddy thought I wasn't happy to see them pictures on account of how I put my head between my knees and cried. But I just wasn't expecting them. All that time I grieved for not having any part of Bobby—not even Pete—to remember him by, it never once crossed my mind that Daddy had a piece. I reckon I was so worried about him not coming back from the war that I never thought he might come and bring a little bit of Bobby with him.

Daddy put his arms around me and rocked me and I hung on to him and sucked in the smell of his cigarettes and his hair tonic. And I felt Momma and the girls hanging on to him and me both.

It wasn't ever going to be like it was before, but at least Bobby had found a way to come back to us.

"Let's go home," I said. All of a sudden I felt like I was going to split wide open if I didn't get there.

When it was just about noon, we pulled into our dirt road. I was sucking it all in—the smell of the red dust we raised as we went down the road, the sight of the honey-suckles in the side ditch, and the little colored church sitting off to the right.

When we come around the last curve in the road, I seen our house sitting there, the same as always. The sun was bouncing off the windows. Momma's roses was blooming out front. And the mimosa tree was covered over in fluffy pink blossoms again.

The vegetable garden was growing up in weeds and someone was out there hoeing. Junior Bledsoe. He pulled off his straw hat and waved it like he was welcoming a soldier home from the war. Then he come a-running.

By the time we was out of the truck, his momma come out of the house and was hugging me like I was her lost puppy dog. "Lord, have mercy! I missed you, girl." She stepped back and looked me up and down. "You need some meat on those bones, and I fixed a big dinner. So you better come and eat."

Junior was waiting behind his momma then, swatting that straw hat against his thigh and studying me, like maybe he thought I was different now.

But I reckon he decided I wasn't—because he put his straw hat on my head and said, "Hey, Ann Fay, you better hurry up and eat some 'taters and fried chicken. That garden needs to be weeded—real bad."

"Well then, Junior Bledsoe," I said, "you and me better crank up that tiller."

BLUE

EPILOGUE

If you ask folks around here what they remember about 1945,

A child might say, "That was the year my daddy come back from the war."

A mother is likely to look you in the eye and declare that polio could not keep us down.

And the *Hickory Daily Record* will say it was the year that the Miracle of Hickory closed its doors.

If anyone knows about them things, it's me, Ann Fay Honeycutt, for sure.

But if you ask me what I remember,

I will say it was the year Franklin D. Roosevelt died and I got one of his flowers.

I will tell you that yellow rose give me the courage to do the right thing even if it was hard.

I will say it was the time in my life when I learned that all of us is fragile as a mimosa blossom.

But the miracle of it all is,

When push comes to shove, we can be just as tough as Hickory.

It mostly hurts at first. After a while it starts to feel better.

BLUE

AUTHOR'S NOTE

What's Real? What's Not?

Polio epidemics were very real and very scary. The first major epidemic in America, affecting tens of thousands of people, came in 1916, and polio returned every summer after that. No one could predict where it would strike.

In 1944, western North Carolina was hit by polio. Health officials chose Hickory as the place to treat patients because it had a camp that could become a hospital.

The emergency hospital expanded from one building to fourteen wards. Sometimes men worked overnight, in the rain, to get the next ward built. Some wards had canvas tent roofs, wooden floors and half-walls, screens on the upper half of the walls, and flaps to keep out rain. As cooler weather came, builders turned the tent wards into permanent buildings.

North Carolina's governor sent prisoners to do laundry and kitchen work. The Red Cross and the March of Dimes recruited doctors and nurses from around the country.

Hickory residents donated lumber, food, blankets, electric fans, and toys. Many volunteered their time and hard work. Reporters from national magazines wrote about "the Miracle of Hickory." The March of Dimes made a movie about the hospital, which showed in theaters across America to raise money to fight polio.

BLUE

Although most public buildings were racially segregated at the time, former patients remember whites and blacks sharing wards. However, the *Hickory Daily Record* refers to a "colored convalescent ward." Apparently the races were separated when they left the contagious ward.

Who Was Real and Who Was Not?

Ann Fay Honeycutt and Imogene Wilfong (and their families and friends) are fictitious characters. Most of the hospital staff is fictitious as well. However, some of the characters were real people who made Hickory's emergency hospital a true miracle.

Dr. H. C. Whims was the county health officer, and Dr. Gaither Hahn was a local physician. Both worked selflessly to establish the hospital and care for polio patients. Mrs. Earle Townsend was making blackberry cobbler for campers when Dr. Whims told her to send the children home. She stayed to cook for patients and hospital staff.

Dr. Dorothy Horstmann was one of three Yale University researchers who came to Hickory to study the spread of polio. Frances Allen was the local public health nurse who visited homes and collected specimens for Yale researchers.

The hot packs that Ann Fay and Imogene endured were the treatment methods of a woman named Sister Elizabeth Kenny. Miss Kenny was an Australian army nurse who pioneered a treatment for polio patients, replacing body casts and splints with moist heat and massage. Australian doctors shunned her methods, so she brought them to the United States. At first American doctors were skeptical, but within a few years many recommended Kenny's methods for restoring mobility to affected muscles.

The little girl named Shelby was a patient at the Hickory

hospital, as was Danny Moury, whose father made a home movie of the hospital. I saw the movie and interviewed Danny and Shelby as well as other patients who shared their memories of the hospital and how it felt to have polio.

Miss Ruth, Ann Fay's physiotherapist, is fictitious, but I named her for a wonderful physical therapist named Ruth who worked during three other polio epidemics and helped me with my research. Her compassion and the twinkle in her eye were very real!

Dr. Robert Bennett was director of physical medicine at the polio rehabilitation center in Warm Springs, Georgia, during this time. He made numerous visits to the Hickory and Charlotte hospitals to assess the progress of patients.

Franklin D. Roosevelt was an active thirty-nine-year-old politician when polio struck him in 1921. He dropped out of politics and focused on trying to walk again. Then in 1924 he visited a resort in Georgia with warm springs. He loved the place so much that he bought it and turned it into a rehabilitation center for people with polio. The next thing "Doctor Roosevelt" knew, he was in the warm pools leading other polios in his favorite water exercises.

But his friends wanted him back in politics, so he interrupted his plans to learn to walk again. He ran for governor of New York and then for president of the United States. As president, he had less time to spend at Warm Springs, but it was still one of his favorite places to relax. He died there on April 12, 1945.

Not everyone agreed with Roosevelt's politics. But he was loved by millions because he cared about the average American and proved that people with disabilities can do great things. Because of his example, America began to see that people with disabilities should have access to the same

BLUE

activities that able-bodied people enjoy.

Even poor Americans like Ann Fay were welcome at Warm Springs. It still operates as a leading rehabilitation center. A visit to quiet Warm Springs offers a look at the Roosevelt Institute for Rehabilitation, the historic warm-water pools, Roosevelt's Little White House, and the FDR State Park.

Polio Today

During the epidemics, Americans were eager to help the March of Dimes, which was begun by Roosevelt and his friends in 1938. Through the President's Birthday Balls and other fundraising events, the organization raised millions of dollars for polio care and increased research.

Since 1908, scientists had known that polio was caused by a virus. In 1952, two scientists (one of them was Dorothy Horstmann) proved that the poliovirus travels in the bloodstream before it attacks the nervous system and causes paralysis. This meant that a vaccine could prevent paralyzing cases of polio. But which scientists would create the vaccine, and how would it work?

Two scientists, Albert Sabin and Jonas Salk, wanted to put a bit of the poliovirus into healthy people. They hoped the body would then produce antibodies to fight the disease. In 1954, when Salk successfully vaccinated children against polio, Americans idolized him. But eventually Sabin's vaccine proved more effective and easier to give, and for decades it replaced Salk's vaccine. Now both are used, in different parts of the world, depending upon the need.

The Western Hemisphere was declared free of polio in 1994, and the World Health Organization is close to ridding the entire world of polio.

Unsolved Mysteries

With the arrival of the vaccine, polio research declined. Polio faded from our memories, and many questions went unanswered. We never learned for sure why polio flared up in summer. We don't know why polio affected a particular area one summer and moved to another the next.

We do know that the poliovirus is passed through contact with human feces. The germs enter the mouth, multiply in the intestine, and then move to the spinal cord, where they may cripple parts of the nervous system. We know that a boy like Bobby might have contacted the virus from the latch on the outhouse door, from a doorknob, or from any person who had the germs on his hands. Since Bobby's twin sisters complained about tummy aches, they could have had mild cases of polio that they got from Bobby and passed on to Ann Fay.

Oh, and What About the Dog?

"Polio Pete" showed up at the emergency hospital during the early part of the epidemic and was adopted by the hospital staff. By mid-August, the *Hickory Daily Record* reported that Pete had gone missing. Later his body was found under one of the hospital buildings.

Newspaper reporters speculated that Pete's master was a patient in the hospital, but no one ever knew whose dog he was. I thought a faithful dog like Pete deserved an adoring owner like Bobby Honeycutt.

Finding the Story

A few years ago I called the director of my local historical association. I told him I'd be attending a history-writing workshop and had an assignment to find an interesting local story. The director suggested the "Miracle of Hickory" and the 1944 polio epidemic.

I hurried to our city library for more information and spent the afternoon reading stories of my townspeople pulling together in a crisis. Right away I wanted to write about this event. I didn't know who my characters would be, but I was excited by a library book I'd found—Alice E. Sink's *The Grit Behind the Miracle*, a nonfiction account of Hickory's polio epidemic and emergency hospital.

Sink's book is filled with events, dates, and important figures. It contains personal stories of patients and staff at the hospital. I quickly learned that all the details of my story were hidden in history itself; I simply had to dig for the details.

Much of my research involved reading old copies of the *Hickory Daily Record*. Like Ann Fay Honeycutt, I found advertisements, war news, and stories about the polio hospital. I traveled to nearby towns to read old issues of *The Charlotte Observer*, *The Charlotte News*, and the *Greensboro Daily News*.

I read books about polio, President Roosevelt, World War II, and racial segregation. I visited historical sites as far apart as Warm Springs, Georgia, and Auschwitz, Poland. I interviewed museum directors, a physical therapist, and patients who'd had polio.

To learn about life in the 1940s, I scanned books about antiques. I listened to old radio shows and forties music. I interviewed senior citizens and World War II vets.

The problem with research is that once I start, I can't seem to stop. I fill my shelves with great books on my subject. I'll mention a few resources that were especially helpful.

Books About Polio

Black Bird Fly Away: Disabled in an Able-Bodied World,
  by Hugh Gregory Gallagher (Vandamere Press, 1998)
Breath: Life in the Rhythm of an Iron Lung, by Martha Mason
  (Down Home Press, 2003)
The Grit Behind the Miracle, by Alice E. Sink
  (University Press of America, 1998)
Healing Warrior: A Story About Sister Elizabeth Kenny,
  by Emily Crofford (Carolrhoda Books, 1989)
In the Shadow of Polio: A Personal and Social History,
  by Kathryn Black (Addison-Wesley, 1996)
Jonas Salk, by Victoria Sherrow (Facts On File, 1993)
March of Dimes, by David W. Rose (Arcadia, 2003)
A Nearly Normal Life, by Charles L. Mee
  (Little, Brown & Co., 1999)
A Paralyzing Fear: The Triumph Over Polio in America,
  by Nina Gilden Seavey, Jane S. Smith, and Paul Wagner
  (TV Books, 1998)
Patenting the Sun: Polio and the Salk Vaccine,
  by Jane S. Smith (William Morrow, 1990)
Polio, by Thomas M. Daniel and Frederick C. Robbins
  (University of Rochester Press, 1997)
Small Steps: The Year I Got Polio, by Peg Kehret
  (Albert Whitman & Co., 1996)
A Summer Plague: Polio and Its Survivors, by Tony Gould
  (Yale University Press, 1995)
And They Shall Walk: The Life Story of Sister Elizabeth Kenny,
  by Elizabeth Kenny (Dodd, Mead & Co., 1943)

Books About Franklin D. Roosevelt, Warm Springs, and the March of Dimes

FDR: My Boss, by Grace Tully (People's Book Club, 1949)
FDR's Last Year: April 1944–1945,
  by Jim Bishop (William Morrow, 1974)
FDR's Splendid Deception: The Moving Story of Roosevelt's Massive
  Disabilities, by Hugh Gregory Gallagher
  (Dodd, Mead & Co., 1985)
Four Billion Dimes, by Victor Cohn
  (Minneapolis Star and Tribune, 1955)
"Hi Ya Neighbor," by Ruth Stevens (Tupper and Love, 1947)
The Roosevelt I Knew, by Frances Perkins (Viking, 1946)
Roosevelt and the Warm Springs Story,
  by Turnley Walker (A. A. Wyn, 1953)

Books About World War II
America at War: 1941–1945, The Home Front,
 by Clark G. Reynolds (Gallery Books, 1990)
Ernie's War: The Best of Ernie Pyle's World War II Dispatches,
 by David Nichols (Random House, 1986)
The Greatest Generation, by Tom Brokaw (Random House, 1998)
World War II: The Axis Assault, 1939–1942, by Douglas Brinkley
 (Times Books, Henry Holt & Co., 2003)
World War II: The Allied Counteroffensive, 1942–1945,
 by Douglas Brinkley (Times Books, Henry Holt & Co., 2003)

Videos
America Goes to War: The Home Front WWII, by Eric Sevareid
 (PBS Anthony Potter Productions, 1990)
Back Then: The Miracle of Hickory, by Richard Eller
 (S. L. Charter Communications, 1997)
The Greatest Generation, by Tom Brokaw
 (NBC News, New Video Group, 1999)
A Paralyzing Fear: The Story of Polio in America, by Nina Gilden
 Seavey (Corporation for Public Broadcasting, 1998)

Fiction
Autumn Street, by Lois Lowry (Houghton Mifflin, 1980)
Close to Home, by Lydia Weaver (Viking, 1993)
Don't You Know There's a War On?, by Avi (HarperCollins, 2001)
Early Sunday Morning: The Pearl Harbor Diary of Amber Billows,
 by Barry Denenberg (Scholastic, 2001)
Hero of Lesser Causes, by Julie Johnston (Lester Publishing, 1992)
The Journal of Ben Uchida: Citizen 13559 Mirror Lake Internment
 Camp, by Barry Denenberg (Scholastic, 1999)
The Journal of Scott Pendleton Collins: A World War II Soldier,
 by Walter Dean Myers (Scholastic, 1999)
Lily's Crossing, by Patricia Reilly Giff
 (Delacorte Books for Young Readers, 1997)
My Last Days as Roy Rogers, by Pat Cunningham Devoto
 (Warner Books, 1999)
My Secret War: The World War II Diary of Madeline Beck,
 by Mary Pope Osborne (Scholastic, 2000)

THE EXPERTS WHO HELPED ME

I discovered this story with the help of many experts and owe a great deal of credit to them. To Carolyn Yoder of Calkins Creek Books, who sent me digging for hidden history and taught me how to write about it. (I never expected to get the nurture of an editor who was so writer-friendly and professionally demanding!) To Patti Gauch for a great writing weekend that took my work to another level, and to Kent Brown and all the folks at The Highlights Foundation for providing the workshops that shaped this story. To Katya Rice, who somehow managed to reconcile Ann Fay's voice with a copy editor's passion for good sentence structure, and to Helen Robinson, who made *Blue* so beautiful. To the experts who helped me understand the effects of polio and the Miracle of Hickory story—John Myer, Shelby Duane, Daniel Moury, Eubert Sigmon, Margaret Hunt, Maria Winkler-Hyams, Inez Sigmon, Ramona Hartzler, John Nyce, and especially Ruth Morton. (Thanks to Ruth, Ramona, John Nyce, and Shelby for reading the manuscript and giving me feedback.) To senior citizens who answered my questions about life during World War II—Hal and Pauline Willis, Jack and Clara Abernethy, Clarence and Irene Lynch, and especially my parents, Wellington and Evangeline Moyer. To Larry Mosteller, who shared his expertise on antique cars, and to Kay for the books on antiques. To Debbie Richey of Sentimental Journey Antiques, for answering my nit-picky questions. To Michael Shaddix, senior librarian at the Roosevelt Warm Springs Institute for Rehabilitation, who shared priceless photos, scrapbooks, and other artifacts, answered questions, and read pertinent parts of the manuscript. To Sydney Halma at the Catawba County Historical Association, who answered numerous questions, made precious archival materials available, and read the manuscript for accuracy. To David W. Rose, archivist for the March of Dimes, who clarified historical information for me. To Carol McCormick of the University of North Carolina Herbarium, for sharing her expertise on North Carolina plant life. To my friends at Patrick Beaver Memorial Library, Catawba County Library, Greensboro Public Library, Davidson University Library, and Tuskegee Institute. To Doris Jean and Anne for their hospitality and help with research. To my writer friends who critiqued my manuscript and held my hand during the breathless waiting—Christine Taylor-Butler, Jen Mann, Kathy Erskine, Vy Armour, and especially Marilyn Hershey, who believed in me when I needed it most. To loved ones who read the manuscript and gave me feedback—Wendy, Kathleen, Joanne, Jeannie, Jessie, Grace, Miriam, Lovena, Elma, Rick, Ruth, Kelly, Kay, and Larry. To Shirley Cunningham, the eighth-grade teacher who forecast my future as a writer, and to David Hazard, who at one of those many writer events affirmed my teacher's predictions. And last but also first, to my husband, Chuck Hostetter, whose expertise lies in loving generously, funding my writing addiction, and listening to the many agonies involved, both mine and those of my characters.

BLUE